D0661821

# The Vampire Gideon's Suicide Hotline & Halfway House for Orphaned Girls

Andrew Katz

LANTERNFISH PRESS
Philadelphia, PA

THE VAMPIRE GIDEON'S SUICIDE HOTLINE AND HALFWAY HOUSE FOR ORPHANED GIRLS



Lanternfish Press
399 Market Street, Suite 360
Philadelphia, PA 19106
lanternfishpress.com

Cover
Design by Michael Norcross.

Printed in the United States of America.
Library of Congress Control Number: 2018942129
ISBN: 978-1-941360-20-0

For Rick and Donna Heaslip,
without whom I would never have actually gotten anything done.

# Chapter One

There is more than one way to build a coffin. Mine is a square, concrete subbasement with a desk, handset telephone, and telemarketer's headset.

The phone rings.

"Hello, suicide hotline. If this is an emergency, please hang up and call 9-1-1, or go to your nearest emergency room."

There are violent sobs on the other end of the phone line.

It is a young man. He is calling me because he cannot let anyone he knows hear him crying. He swears he is not in danger. He just needs to talk without being judged.

I could tell him to talk to someone he knows. To hang up on me and call his parents. Call a friend. Call someone who can tell him about their day. Just something to take his mind off a lonely night.

But that would not be professional.

He swears to me, again, that he is not in any immediate danger.

"It's from this weekend. I think I'm just overwhelmed. There's this girl that I'm . . . that I'm friends with."

He is sobbing the whole time. Ragged breaths break up every third or fourth word.

He says, "I'm pretty sure I'm in love with her."

He is in love with her.

"But we're friends." His voice bubbles with snot. "And I think she liked me once. I was really fat, though. With, like, mega-low self-esteem. And I missed my chance."

His voice reaches a pitch of near-hysteria.

"I'm just so fucking stupid. This is so fucking stupid. Calling you, a total stranger, was so fucking stupid."

I listen to the silence for a three count.

He says, "I think . . . I think maybe I should just kill myself."

He sounds in need of a kind tone, not an ambulance. However, when it comes to dying, you can never be too careful.

"You are not stupid," I say.

"Yes, I am!" he shouts.

I wait. The only sound coming through is sobbing.

"You are not stupid," I say. "You are human. Things are challenging. Stress tolerance is difficult to develop. It gets easier as you get older."

"I'm old enough," he whines. "Twenty-four and I have absolutely nothing to show for my life. When do things become okay? Where's my goddamn fucking 'king me' moment?"

Jiminy Christmas. Twenty-four years old. No different than the angst of fourteen. You just think you know more.

"I am almost a century older than you. I am still not old enough."

He snorts. The sound of his popping snot bubble fills the headset.

My dead ears hear everything that happens on the other end of the phone line. I do not know if the sensitive hearing is a result of my physical condition or if it is a matter of attention.

When you are dead, it is important to focus on things that count.

I tell him, "I am a vampire."

"A—a vampire?"

"Yes."

His sobs strangle him. "Oh, oh my God. You're not even taking this seriously, are you? I can't believe I'm that stupid. Oh, my God. I can't believe I called and you're just making fun of me."

He hangs up.

Most of the time they pick up the phone again. To call me, perhaps. To call their family or friends. To call 9-1-1.

I sit at my desk chair, motionless. When there is no blood pumping through your body it is very easy to remain still. The impossible thing is to keep your mind in the same state. I think about what I will say to this young man if and when he calls back.

I figure it out.

The phone does not ring.

I receive several more calls over the course of the night. None of the callers sounds particularly endangered. Two are mentally ill, calling from within the hospital to chat. Neither thinks that I am making fun of them when I say I am a vampire.

The so-called mentally ill are often much more perceptive than their "sane" counterparts. They can smell deceit from 20,000 leagues under the sea. Perhaps that is what makes them lose their minds in the first place. They have to deal with all the liars.

Try holding onto your mind when nothing you hear is true.

✦ ✦ ✦

The next night starts off with a sixteen-year-old victim of sexual abuse. I tell her it is not her fault. She is skeptical.

I ask, "Have you tried to reach out to anyone about this?"

I hear a rustle as she shakes her head. "No one wants to listen to teenage girls. They think we're all, like, totally fucking crazy."

I ask her if she wants me to contact anyone.

She gives an emphatic *no*.

She says, "If he touches me one more time, I don't think I'll make it through."

She is not crying. Something tells me she is long past suffering out loud.

I tell her she will make it through. I tell her that no amount of pain is worth dying for. I tell her life is never so bad if you can survive it.

She says she doesn't really feel like surviving it. She sounds almost bored.

I tell her that none of what is happening to her is her fault.

She tells me she knows that.

I do not believe her.

I say, "Confronting difficult emotions is better than wishing you could feel anything at all."

"I can't say I really agree. I think I like not feeling anything. That way I'm not so worried if I'll ever get to be happy. I'm not so sure happiness, like, exists. Not for everyone, anyway. And I don't think that, if maybe it does, it's really attainable. You know? Or at least not how we've been taught. Like, this ideal form of happiness they show you in rom-coms or *Twilight*. Where the lowest they experience is their 'person' leaving them. Their 'soulmate.' But, like, even then, it's only so they can realize they need each other, and that one small low is all they need to, like, remember forever that their relationship is the greatest high that exists in the whole universe."

I make a sound of affirmation.

"So, what I'm getting at—thanks for letting me ramble, by the way—is, what's the point of your relative high if you're stuck in a low so fucking deep that even the donkey trying to bring you to the top of the canyon is too depressed to start walking?"

I say, "You go on living."

"That's it?"

"It is the only thing to do."

"But it sucks mule cock."

"Do you mind if I divulge some personal information? I do not wish to take the focus off of you, but I believe that hearing about another person's experience may help with what you are going through."

I hear her thinking.

She says, "Sure. Advice is like a buffet anyway. You take what you want and leave the rest on the fucking table."

"Quite," I say. "I am dead. And have been so for over seventy years."

Silence on the other end. I let the notion percolate.

"What do you mean you're dead?"

"I mean that I am dead. And have been brought back. Your popular culture would characterize me as a vampire, although I find the legends associated with such creatures to be rather sensational and inaccurate."

"Okay, fuckface, I don't know if this is your way of lightening the fucking mood or what, but say I even believed you, what's that got to do with, like, anything?"

"Because I can tell you without a shadow of a doubt that dying is worse than any possible outcome of living. When people tell you there are fates worse than death, they are speaking from a necessarily uninformed position. They have not experienced it. If they had, they would never be able to utter those words with any confidence."

"You're definitely fucking with me now."

"Not at all." I laugh. "In point of fact, I find a large part of the modern vampire's obsession with sex to be utterly silly. My object is to conserve blood, not to waste it inflating an organ that is only useful to the living."

She gives a haughty snort. "I always thought that was weird. Corpses fucking, I mean. Is all that hypnotism stuff true?"

"More or less. Back to the point. Vampirism is all about food. Trying to succeed in surviving when we have already failed so miserably. Sex doesn't much enter into the equation."

"So what *is* your point?"

"You don't know anything, yet. And you will not. Ever. Not really. That does not hinder the beauty of learning and growing and persevering. Take my word for it. Dying, and I will choose here from a lexicon of which you seem fond, 'like, totally fucking sucks.' It is the worst. I have done it. I know."

Another snort.

She says, "I live with a foster father. He carries a sock with a Master lock in it."

She says, "He knocks me unconscious with it when I fight him."

She says, "He's a fucking asshole, but I have nowhere else to go."

I ask her, "May I tell you a story?"

✦ ✦ ✦

I am thirty-one. The year predates cell phones and the internet. It is between the two world wars. Those are the only relevant cultural changes between then and now. Everything else is the same with different names.

It is winter. I am in a wool coat. I am still alive. The sun is up, though veiled by gray clouds. I take its presence for granted. I am walking to my destination in a poor neighborhood. The houses are built in rows, sharing exterior walls. None of this is particularly important, but when you tell a story it is good to set the occasional scene.

I am on my way to see a girl. When you are as old as I am, everyone from the past is a boy or girl. No one has enough perspective to be considered a man or woman. These words imply a level of experience most human beings cannot hope to attain.

We are all nothing more than children until we die.

I walk into the building. There is no doorman nor reception desk. It is the kind of housing in which people are expected to look out for themselves.

The girl I am going to see is impoverished and lives on the twelfth floor. Wealthier people live lower, so they do not have to climb as many steps. The atmosphere grows bleaker the higher I go. There is no fairy-tale penthouse atop this building.

The stairwells have frayed carpeting and peeling wallpaper. The walls are thin and you hear almost everything. Including ear-piercing screams. And thuds. The sounds of future bruises and cracked ribs.

I get to the twelfth floor.

"Hello," I say when the girl opens the door.

Her hair is dark and curly. Eyes the pale blue of glacial water. Her dimples are deep and her teeth very white. Her face is a wonder to look upon. She appears surprised to see me. She clears her throat. She is not dressed to go out. She is barely dressed at all.

She asks me why I'm here.

I tell her we have plans.

She says, "Oh. Was that today?"

"Yes."

She does not invite me in. I stand there awkwardly.

I ask, "Are we going out?"

She looks over her shoulder. A large boy comes to the door behind her. He is shirtless. He is more muscular than I am. He is at least four inches taller. He has a cruel face and aggression set in his shoulders.

"The fuck are you?" he asks.

Keep in mind that at this time, profanity is a much less accepted form of speech among the educated and the unschooled alike. I do not believe this boy is the former. Of course, I only have one year of university to my name, having dropped out some time ago.

I tell him my name. He tilts his head at me and rests his hands on the girl's hips, pressing her against him. She looks up at him.

I clear my throat. The boy is staring at me.

"We had plans," I say.

He presses a thumb against his barrel chest. "We had plans?"

My voice turns weak and light. "She and I."

He laughs. His laughter is as ignoble as his eyes. He pulls her tighter against him. She lets out a little gasp.

He says, "Me and her have plans. You don't fit in them."

My manhood threatened, my survival instincts flare. *Make yourself big to fend off predators.*

"Maybe *you* don't fit into *our* plans." My voice cracks as I say it. He pulls the girl closer against himself.

He says, "I fit just fine."

In my youth, I was prone to impulsivity; now that I am immortal, I tend to think before acting. You might expect the contrary to be true, but experiencing the enormity of death creates a certain reflectiveness.

I laugh in his face.

He does not like this. He tells me he doesn't care for the way I articulate my words. He says he has half a mind to teach me a lesson.

I say, "If you were a teacher, I would feel sincerely concerned for the future of mankind."

This is the wrong thing to say.

He throws the girl aside. He grips me by the lapels of my coat and drags me inside. My struggling is ineffectual, to say the least. He goes about savagely beating me. He throws his fists into the side of my head and ribs. He kicks at my rear and back. I make myself as small as possible to try and placate him.

The girl grabs the boy's elbow in a futile attempt to restrain him. He elbows her back. She falls on the floor, knees to her chest, and cries.

No one will call the police in this building.

Once I am sufficiently defeated, the boy turns back to the girl. He grips her by the upper arm and tosses her onto the bed. It groans and squeaks in protest. The boy slams the door shut. You can already see his erection straining the fabric of his pants as he unbuckles his belt.

My entire body thrums to the beat of my heart. The pain pounds with every thump. My mouth is clotted with blood and my eyes are blurry with tears. These conditions do not dull the experience of seeing the boy grab the girl through her crying protests.

He proceeds to rape her.

He turns back to me afterward. The girl is crying. She crawls off the bed to jam herself between its frame and the wall. I am having trouble breathing. The boy leans down close to my face. His breath smells like stale beer and rotten meat.

He asks me, "You learn something now?"

Weakly, I spit blood at his feet. It is not an intentional act of defiance. It is so that I can breathe. Predictably, he does not see it this way.

He takes me by an ankle, drags me through the door, and rolls me down the stairs.

At this point, shock has set in. I am shaking on the landing between the eleventh and twelfth floors, soaking the ragged carpet with my blood.

✦ ✦ ✦

The girl asks, "Is that it?"

I tell her, "Yes."

"Is that supposed to make me feel better?"

"Not yet."

"Then *why fucking tell me?*"

"The world is not pretty. It is not neat. It is work to be alive. Work that has immeasurable value. Do you know what I did after this encounter?"

"What?"

"I went on living. Do you know what the girl from the story did?"

"No."

"She went on living. Do you know what the boy from the story did?"

"He went on living?"

"No. He died horribly. I can guarantee you, nothing he experienced was ever worse. And now he has no way to repent for his sins. Whether God exists or not, he was punished."

"How do you know that?"

I do not tell her.

Instead I say, "Because he never grew into anything better than what he was. He forced his way through the world. People like that, well, they eventually run into something bigger than themselves."

"But it sounds like nothing happened to him. Everyone dies. The girl will die. You'll die. We all die. Why can't I just do it now? If it'll happen when I'm seventy, why shouldn't I just get it out of the way?"

"Because your antagonist will die first. By living you are exacting the utmost form of revenge. By showing him that no matter how he hurts you, he can never break you. Cruelty is born from the need to see others suffer into nonexistence."

I ask her if she wants me to contact anyone on her behalf.

She gives an emphatic *no.*

✦ ✦ ✦

The sixteen-year-old's home is in a neighborhood like that of the girl whom I used to know. I cannot enter without an invitation, but mostly because the door is locked. This is not a huge problem. I buzz every tenant in turn.

Most do not answer. Four do.

The first is an angry-sounding boy who—upon hearing my lie about having an urgent package for him from the government—tells me to go fuck myself.

The second is a girl of similar demeanor and response.

The third is a boy who does not recognize my voice and apologetically tells me he doesn't want whatever I'm selling before I can say more than "hello."

The fourth is a gift from on High, or Low, if you believe in that sort of thing. An old girl, who sounds senile and hopeful. I tell her I am her son come to visit. It is not a nice thing to do. Such is life.

She squeals, "Come in!"

The door buzzes, magnetic lock disengaging. I open it. I stop at the old girl's room and knock. The door creaks open. The old girl stands in the threshold, eyes rheumy, hair long and silver. She looks at me for a long time.

She says, "Theodore!"

"Miss Havisham," I say.

"Hmm? Speak up, your mother doesn't hear so well these days."

I say, "Mother, it is a pleasure to see you."

"Come in, come in."

I follow her into her apartment. The domicile is a cliché, to say the least. There are sofas with slipcovers, doilies on the armrests, a coffee table upon which sit wilted flowers. There is a pot of water boiling on a stove to the left of the sitting room. Miss Havisham bustles over to the stove.

I sit at her small kitchen table with its floral cloth.

"Theodore," she croons. "How have you been?"

"Well—"

"Hold that thought, dear. Duty calls." Miss Havisham lets out a cackle and waddles away to her bathroom.

I pace her apartment. On the wall behind the sofa is a black-and-white marriage portrait of a much younger Miss Havisham and a man dressed in formal US Navy garb. They both sport dimples and their smiles seem genuine. Beside the portrait is another with the couple and a teenaged boy. He looks nothing like me.

The toilet flushes. Miss Havisham walks back into her dining room. She screams.

"Who are you?" she asks.

"I am your son, Theodore."

"You're not Theodore! Someone, help!"

Her cries turn to wordless wailing. I leave the room with some haste. From two floors up I hear doors fly open.

A boy calls out, "Shut the fuck up. I don't want to have to tell you again."

A girl shouts, "Can someone quiet that bitch down? I can't take this every night."

The shouts draw others. No one comes to Miss Havisham's defense.

I wonder what a natural aging process would have done to me. It is possible that such a life would be much worse than the one I have come to know.

If only I believed that.

I proceed up the stairs once the din has died out. This is the kind of building with ragged carpeting and peeling wallpaper. With audible screams and thuds. If it could still pump, my heart would send blood rushing to my ears.

I hear the distinct wet burp of a drunk. His is the first door I try; it has crooked numbers. I knock. He opens. The apartment is one room, with a ripped sofa and small, boxy television.

"The fuck are you?" he asks, gassing me with a second burp.

I ask, "Do you foster a daughter?"

He is taken aback. "Who wants to know?"

I look him hard in the eye. His jaw goes slack. "Do you foster a daughter?"

His listing head shakes no. A shame.

I move on.

I hear a fist strike a wall. There is a sharp intake of breath. The stairs whip away beneath my feet. I get to the apartment. This door does not bother with numbers at all.

I pound on it.

A boy shouts, "Go away."

His voice is edged with sandpaper and the smell of bourbon wafts from beneath the door. I keep pounding. There is no need to fear knuckles or small hand bones breaking. (I do not know what part of dying eternalizes you this way. I have never felt the need to question it.) From within the apartment, the boy loudly inquires what the fuck I could possibly want. Heavy footsteps approach the door. In the blink of an eye I am waiting on the landing above.

The door flies open. The boy leans into the hall. He has the look of someone who does not wash often. His face is covered with dirty stubble. He is wearing a short-sleeved bowling shirt with two broad stripes down the chest.

The sixteen-year-old is curled in the far corner of the apartment. Her eye is black and her arms are crosshatched with scars.

This observation takes about a second and a half. The boy is still leaning out the door. He looks both ways.

There is a way to enter a place without an invitation.

Before he can react, I grab him by the shoulder and clamp his lips shut with my thumb and forefinger, dragging him out of his apartment and down to the lower landing. His throat bulges. A scream dies there.

The girl steps around the door frame; her eyes are a glacial blue and her greasy hair is curly. She is wearing a T-shirt several sizes too large with holes at the hem and armpit. Her jeans are in the same state. She watches me. Her foster father looks back and forth between us. His eyes bulge, resembling a panicked fly's.

The girl's face is blank, tired. She walks back into the apartment and shuts the door. I spin her foster father around. A small whine escapes. Before he can cry for help, I have him in a rear-naked chokehold with my hand over his mouth. He loses consciousness. I leave with him slung over my shoulder.

No penthouse, but maybe the ending of a fairy tale, after all.

✦ ✦ ✦

I check my phone. There are thirteen missed calls; I have no answering service. I hope no one committed suicide.

I sit down and place the headset over my brittle hair.

The phone rings several times. None of the calls requires immediate action. I try to lie to a repeat caller named Rich. He catches me every time.

"I was a good man once," I tell him.

He mumbles, "Lie."

"I did a good thing tonight, at least."

He asks me what I did. I tell him about it in reasonable detail.

He says, "Not a good thing."

I ask why not.

He asks me where the man is now.

"Safe."

"Lie."

I say, "What do you know about it, anyway?"

He tells me that he hasn't died, but he knows what it sounds like when death lurks. He sounds sad.

"Might look good now," he says. "Never is."

Rich is often my moral compass.

I tell him I'm getting better about the violence.

"Lie."

I tell him my actions aren't so brutal anymore.

"Lie."

I tell him only the living get to feel emotions.

He scoffs.

I tell him that I am certain the girl's life and the world at large will be better off because of what I have done.

"Lie."

I tell him to suck a penis.

"It sounds weird like that. Try 'eat a dick' instead."

I tell him to eat a dick.

He says no. "Not even you do that. You're always saying it: 'Male genitals are not vampire Slim Jims.'"

I sigh. "Things will eventually get better for us."

He says, "True. But you're still lying."

Rich will spend his life in Saint Augustine's Behavioral Center or a series of places with the same purpose. We talk every other night or so. He smashes his head against the wall if they try to stop him from calling me.

He is probably my best friend.

✦ ✦ ✦

Later that night the twenty-four-year-old boy calls me back. His voice sounds strangled. He is trying to keep from crying.

"I am glad to hear from you again," I say.

"I can't keep doing this, day in, day out," he says. "I can't keep killing time. And do you know the worst part? Do you know?"

He waits for a reply. I ask him what.

"I have no actual problems, whatsoever. I have a good group of friends. I have a decent job. Girls like me . . . well, all except the one I care about, anyway. So sure, I know I'm being dramatic. You know what? It doesn't matter. Knowing that doesn't make me feel even a tiny bit better."

"What does make you feel better?"

Running a suicide hotline often equates to playing armchair psychologist.

"Nothing," he complains. "Nothing makes me feel better. Do you want to know the most fucked-up part?"

I refrain from guessing.

"Even when I think I've had fun, which I guess I do, sometimes, I get home and there's this voice in my head. This tiny, evil thing. And it asks me, 'But did you?' That tiny, malicious question is all I need to tell me that I haven't."

"Have you tried meditating?"

"Yes," he growls. It brings the sobs through. "I run in the morning. I meditate. I've changed my diet. Nothing works. I do everything everyone tells me. I went to college. I got a job. Everything. The whole shebang. The millennial American dream. I'm still not—" he chokes on his own fear of the word "—happy."

I tell him he cannot change unless he really wants to.

He bursts out with a sardonic laugh. "Thanks for the psychology degree, professor."

"It is a harsh truth."

He is not really listening to me. "I have this dark, nebulous thing inside me," he says. "Weighing on me. And talking. It manifests the worst right about now. It—" he sucks in a deep breath "—hurts. So badly."

It is 3:00 a.m. The hour that supposedly tries men's souls. Unfortunately, time has nothing to do with it.

"That's my problem," he says. "I'm fighting with myself. All the time. So obviously, I'm evenly matched with my opponent. Never getting anywhere with anything. It's like there's another Jacob inside of me—" this is how I learn his name "—who I fucking *hate*. I *despise* him. Really and truly. I think of it like a boxing match. There's me, and then there's me with a goatee. We're in the ring, I'm in white trunks, my doppelganger's in red. We throw punches and every single one collides with the other's fist because we think exactly the same. But the only way to kill him is to kill me. I'd be doing the world a favor, really. Getting rid of that kind of evil."

The crying overtakes him.

I say, "You do not deserve to die."

I let him go on crying for a while. There is nothing I can say at the moment to help him.

"Guess what I'm doing right now. Go on. Guess."

I say, "Lying in bed. Crying. Fighting with yourself."

He told me as much already.

He goes into great detail about making a "MacGyver-esque" noose with which to hang himself in his basement. He stops crying. He says, "I'm standing in the noose right now."

He stops crying.

"Jacob," I say. "I need you to listen to me. You are focused, far too heavily, on the one way you are feeling at this moment. Yes?"

He gulps.

"Okay. You say you have a group of friends. What would this action accomplish? Hurting them. Or your family. Suicide will not end your pain, only pass it along."

"Who would I even pass it to? No one gives a shit whether I live or die. That's the whole reason I'm down here."

"Do you have parents?" I ask.

"Yeah."

"As a parent myself, I can assure you, there is nothing worse than the loss of a child."

He scoffs. "I haven't talked to my parents in weeks."

"Why not?"

"I don't know. They're always calling to check up on me. It's smothering. It's awful. It's like they're so constantly worried about me that there's no trust left."

"In their defense," I say, "it seems there may be good reason to worry. Given your current predicament, that is."

He sniffs mucus. There is a pregnant pause in which I can almost hear the gears turning in his head. He says, "That makes sense."

"Take the noose off, Jacob."

I hear him do it. There is a tense moment in which I picture him slipping while trying to free himself and dying anyway.

He does not.

"Jacob, thank you for doing that. Are you willing to call 9-1-1 or visit your nearest emergency room?"

I hear him shake his head. "No."

"I told you last time you called that I am dead. Yes?"

"Yes," he croaks.

"And you did not believe me."

"I'm not stupid."

He was standing in a noose a moment ago. Despite this, I do not beg to differ. "Are you a reader, Jacob?"

"Sometimes."

"Are you familiar with the writings of one Samuel Langhorne Clemens?"

"Huh?"

"Mark Twain."

"Oh. Yeah, sure. The guy who wrote that racist book with the kid on the raft."

I clear my throat. "Yes. Fine. He also wrote a book called *A Connecticut Yankee in King Arthur's Court*. Do you know it?"

"No."

Children.

"The plot is not the point, I suppose. There is a rather short passage in the novel. It comes amidst the center of a paragraph. It reads, 'You can't depend on your eyes when your imagination is out of focus.'"

"What's that got to do with anything?"

"Your perspective is limited by your own beliefs. Humans have believed in and written about vampires in one form or another since there have been humans and writing. Why should we be any less possible than you?"

"I don't know, man. You don't seem, uh, evil, or however vampires are supposed to be."

If he only knew the half of it.

"Jacob, there is nothing that will happen to you in life that is worse than dying. You can take my word for that. It is terrible. Or at the very least, incredibly boring."

"Yeah?"

"Yeah. It is really a kick in the proverbial dick, if you catch my drift."

He laughs. "That sentence doesn't sound right coming out of your mouth."

"How so?"

"I don't know. The way you say stuff. It's so proper. The word *dick* sounds wrong with that voice."

My brow furrows. "I have a computer. I read this internet of which you are all so fond. How did you find my number?"

"Google."

"Right. So, I may be very old, but that does not mean I have stopped learning."

"You should tell that to the Republicans."

"They are children still."

He laughs again. It is a boisterous, pleasant sound. "If you say so. The description you put on your webpage, about how nothing we say gets recorded or anything. Is that true?"

"Yes."

"Do you have some kind of license to do this?"

"No."

"Hasn't anyone come and tried to shut you down or anything?"

I think about that. "There is a reason my number does not appear until the twelfth page of an internet search."

"Probably not too good for business. You should get your SEO game up."

"SEO?"

"Search engine optimization."

"Why would I do that?"

He sighs. "To get more calls, duh."

"I am here for the desperate. A last line of defense, if you will, for those who are still willing to talk. To hear that it could be worse. They could be locked in a basement away from the sun for all eternity, for example."

"Dude. That was super bleak. Also, you need to update your website, it looks terrible."

I ask if I may tell him a story.

✦ ✦ ✦

I am thirty-two. The girl—Rachael is her name—still lives in the same apartment.

I walk with a cane now and wear a back brace. I hobble up the stairs and rap on her door with the handle of the cane, steadying myself with a hand on the doorframe.

She opens the door. "Come in."

I do, trying to lessen my limp. I hope to fool her. I know I do not.

Gingerly, I lower myself into a chair at her small, round table. A chunk of wood props it up where the boy broke one of its legs. Rachael takes a teapot from the stove along with two small cups and sits across from me.

Her eyes are still a bright, arctic blue. Her hair is still thick, dark, and curly. Her chin is just weak enough to make her rosy cheeks stand out on the rare occasions left for which she smiles. The damage done to her has been internal.

She is beautiful. No one makes the right decision every time. She is still beautiful. I come over twice a week to tell her these facts. Once out of every four or five times I say it, she smiles. Each time she does, I make sure to tell her again. We drink tea in the intense silence that now haunts the apartment. Neither of us has much to say anymore. Neither of us needs to say much anymore. Neither of us likes the apartment anymore.

We are determined not to let memories kill us.

The boy has moved on. After my crumpled body was collected from the landing by neighbors or the police—I cannot remember which and it does not matter—the boy hit the road. Rachael has not heard from him.

She does not have me over because I make her feel safe. All things considered, this is a given. She has me over because we did have plans that tragic day. I have no intention of breaking them.

Rachael thanks me for coming each time I arrive. After she thanks me for coming, she apologizes. I tell her not to worry. I never say I forgive her; she is not mine to forgive, nor would my forgiveness help anyone. The only one left who can absolve her is herself. God, perhaps.

She says, "I don't want to be around anyone; I just can't be alone, either."

I work as a shipping clerk at my father's company. I am on a leave of absence.

She works nights as a nurse.

The doctors tell her she desperately needs to improve her bedside manner.

A baby cries, easily heard through the thin walls of the building. We sip our tea. She places her hand over mine. Our brokenness makes sure it is the most touching we ever do.

✦ ✦ ✦

Jacob says, "I don't understand."

"It is a parable."

"Thanks," he drawls. "I mean I don't understand what it has to do with me."

Because, obviously, the world revolves around him.

"It is important for all the years it has stuck with me. It is important because that is a most treasured memory. When I grow too unhappy, I think about it. It lessens the pain of the moment. It refocuses me. You have pleasant memories, yes?"

"I guess so."

"I am going to give you homework," I say.

"What?"

"Homework. A thing for you to do at home. That will be useful to you."

"You're real fucking condescending, you know that?"

"Yes."

He tells me that's exactly what he's talking about.

"I want you to think of a memory. Not a great accomplishment. Something small. A day outdoors when you did not feel quite so anxious. So frustrated."

"I don't know if I've had one of those. Not for a long time."

I say, "Think about it. Something will come up. Then call me in two days. Can you promise me this?"

"Um, sure, I guess."

Giving them tasks gives them something to look forward to. Even if it only buys a little time.

Jacob hangs up.

I stand, limbs cracking. I have been still for a long time this night. My living space is empty aside from the desktop computer, the desk, and the phone. There is a side room with a bed in which I sleep. I have learned that as long as I am away from the sun, I am safe.

Beside my bed is a radiator installed by the former owner, who disappeared under mysterious circumstances. Chained to the radiator is a small girl's former foster father. He is already looking slightly emaciated.

Talking children down from nooses is hungry work.

The boy's eyes bulge. He whimpers. Begs for freedom. No one can hear him down here.

He spent his first night screaming his throat raw.

I bite him about the wrist. He cries out. He has an iron deficiency, for sure. High cholesterol. Tastes vaguely of cheap hamburgers. He will need food soon, but he is not in immediate peril of starving. I feed until he grows weak and quiet.

Some men do not deserve their blood.

Pondering whether or not I deserve his, I fall asleep.

# Chapter Two

Rich calls.

I answer as I always do. He cuts me off halfway.

"Hello."

"Yellow," I reply in a nasal caricature of his own greeting.

He asks me if my hostage is dead yet.

"No."

He says, "Good. Let him go."

"I will. Eventually."

"Lie."

"I am getting tired of you saying that."

"Lie."

That is the thing about friends.

Rich asks, "You feed him? Not just on him."

"He does not deserve food."

There is a dull silence.

He says, "You believe the wrong things."

"You bang your head against pillars to punish yourself."

"I'm repenting."

I blow air through my nose for effect. "You have suffered enough."

"Honest. Still wrong."

I tell him I'm rarely wrong.

"Lie."

I tell him my intentions are usually good.

"Lie."

I ask him if I should be more penitent.

"Yes."

I tell him there is no God.

I tell him that I died.

I tell him if there were a God, I would have met Him/Her/Them/It.

"Lie."

I ask him what kind of sadist would make my pain last forever.

"This is penance. You don't take it seriously."

I tell him I take it as seriously as I can.

"Lie."

I tell him I do my best to help.

"Sometimes."

I ask him how he is doing.

He says, "Talk soon."

✦ ✦ ✦

The sixteen-year-old girl calls. Her name is Margie.

"You took him."

"What?"

"Don't fuck with me. You took him. I told you to not, like, call anyone."

"I obeyed your wish."

"It meant I didn't need help."

"You called worried you would kill yourself."

"I was just *venting*. What is wrong with you?"

"How are you?"

"I haven't been back to school or anything, so it's been pretty chill. I don't have any other kids, like, picking on me or whatever. But so, I don't know. I don't know what I'm supposed to *do* anymore. That's giving me some anxiety. But also it's kind of a relief, I guess."

"Are you fed? Watered? Sheltered?"

"Yeah. For now, anyway. But I don't really have much money. Jerry keeps a can on top of the fridge for beer and whiskey and cigarettes and weed and whatever. There's a bunch of canned soup and baked beans and Tastykakes here. So I've been eating those."

"Would you like for me to contact Children's Services for you?"

"God, you're annoying."

"I am doing my best not to be."

"Well, you're failing."

"I apologize."

"Whatever. Look, I don't know what you did to him, and part of me couldn't care any less, but there's like another part of me that kind of wants to know. You know?"

"He is safe."

She snorts. "You were pissed. I saw you."

"I do not agree. I was simply trying to help you."

"You know that I'm sixteen, right?"

"Yes."

"So I'm not exactly an adult."

"Neither is Jerry. Parents are just children in charge of smaller children. You are more suited to raise yourself at this point, I believe."

"Did you kill him?"

"No."

"Then where is he?"

I say, "You should go to school."

She sighs. "I know. But the fucking guidance counselors are always calling me to their offices. They want to know how I'm doing. I don't tell them anything, and they can't really do anything about it because I get good grades."

"How long have you been self-harming?"

Her defense is instantaneous. "How long have you been a vampire?" she asks.

All my life.

I say, "For about seventy years."

"Wow. Have you, like, killed a bunch of people?"

"No. Killing someone is the ultimate evil. Dying is—" I affect an imitation of her voice "—like, the worst, or whatever."

Her voice goes deadpan. "I do *not* sound like that."

"Like, totally not, I guess."

"Stop it."

"Like, if you say so, or whatever, I guess."

"You're *so* annoying."

"I do my best to lighten moods when it feels appropriate."

She says she isn't feeling particularly light. She says once someone figures out she's on her own they'll throw her into another bad situation. She says that Anne Frank book they teach you is total horseshit because sure, maybe some people are inherently good, but definitely not all of them.

She goes on for a long time about how school shouldn't fill kids' minds with unattainable ideals. She says if she were Anne Frank she really would have killed herself. She says that stupid twat was so naïve, and clearly her family was too rich to teach her anything real.

I ask if I may tell her a story.

✦ ✦ ✦

I am thirty-three. Rachael and I have become what current psychologists describe as codependent. We spend most of each day together, discussing politics or philosophy or the weather.

We say "I love you" to one another whenever we part ways. I am working again. With my back, manual labor is out of the question. Still, with an active mind and a chip on your shoulder, you can accomplish most anything. I tell her about my work. She tells me about hers.

A man gropes her backside one day. She comes home and cries for hours.

Another day we sit on a park bench. A small boy runs in the near distance with the wobbling exuberance that only toddlers have. Rachael has brought food for the pigeons.

"I hate that you feed these winged rodents," I say.

She pats my shoulder. "I know, dear."

"Why do you do it?"

"Their lives are as important as ours."

"They are not even self-aware."

"Neither are you, most of the time."

I blow a raspberry at her. She giggles.

She chides, "How mature."

I stretch out in autumn's afternoon sun. "No one is perfect."

Then, as if summoned, our antagonist appears. He is as large as ever, with stubble stretching down his neck. He wears an undershirt tucked into black slacks. A heavy silver chain with a crucifix on it hangs glittering at his breast.

He stops before our bench, sneers.

"Look at this shit," he says.

Behind him walks another man, smaller but dressed in the same type of outfit. This man has the appearance of a cruel rat, hair shorn close to his scalp, with a wiry build. Rachael cowers and jams her shoulder into my armpit.

I stare up.

"Please leave," I say.

Rat Face stands behind the rapist and slightly to the side. Rat Face asks, "You got a problem?"

I say, "Yes."

They exchange a look.

The rapist says, "Ya didn't learn your lesson, then?"

I lurch to my feet. "No."

Love makes you brave. Stronger than you were. Our attacker jams a finger into my chest.

"Sit back down," he says.

I am acutely aware of the police officer sitting on a bench opposite us, observing the scene with a professional curiosity.

"I do not think I will. Your face offends me. Your presence is an affront."

Rachael places a hand on my wrist. She tells me we should go.

I look down at her with anger. Her fear and sadness are palpable. Turning back to the two boys, I point out the officer. I tell them it would not be wise to beat up a cripple and a woman in front of an authority figure.

I call the rapist what he is and tell him he is a piece of human filth.

I call him a Neanderthal.

I call him a coward.

It is this last insult that sticks in his craw. It is what draws his right hand to my chin. It is what calls the officer to action.

The invalid, lying on the ground in front of the woman he loves.

Our antagonist hits the police officer. Suddenly three more are upon him and his associate. They beat the two of them with billy clubs. Kick them in the ribs and shoulders. Cuff their arms behind their backs.

The boy who hit me swears his vengeance.

I spit in his face. This time not for my own health.

The officer whom he hit laughs.

I lower myself back onto the bench as the officers take the two away.

Rachael recoils from my attempt to place an arm around her shoulders. She whispers, "Take me home."

I do.

✦ ✦ ✦

Margie asks, "Is that supposed to convince me that people get what they deserve?"

"It is meant to show you that some actions are not appreciated by those for whom we do them, no matter what our intentions may be."

"So why wasn't your girlfriend happy he was gone?"

I tell her that what I did, deep down, had nothing to do with Rachael.

I tell her that my pride is what drove me.

I tell her that in that moment I was really only considering myself.

"Okay, but then, I should, like . . . what?"

"You should consider how your actions affect others."

"What about you, then? You left me all on my own."

"Have you considered why?"

"Because you're just as self-centered as you were back then."

I sigh, wondering if she and Rich would get along. I say, "Maybe. However, you seem strong and resilient. These are extraordinarily valuable qualities. Because of this, I wish the best for you. Jerry was not that."

She ponders this for a long time. "But what should I do now?"

"Go to your school. Use all his money. Consider a job. You may even be able to declare your own adulthood. Develop a plan. Call me in two days to discuss it. But only if you have gone back to your studies."

To my immense relief, she says she will.

She asks me if I became a vampire to take vengeance upon those who wronged me.

"I just wanted a way to live forever, so that I could see the other side of despair. But I am dead, and there is no cure for that."

✦ ✦ ✦

Jerry is in terrible need of food. There is a bodega not far from my home. The clerk, after a moderate amount of hypnotic persuasion, allows me to leave with a paper bowl full of nachos. I return to my subbasement with the food, a gallon of water, and two dog bowls.

Jerry stares as I enter. His stomach grumbles loudly at the smell of food.

I dump the nachos into one bowl and fill the other with water. I set them at his feet and unchain one hand. He punches me weakly across the face, a feeble cross. I slap him hard enough to quell him but not hard enough to break his neck. He spits at my feet.

His bowling shirt is dirty and rumpled. He has soiled himself several times.

I say, "Eat."

He says, "Fuck you."

I say, "No thank you," and return to my desk.

The phone rings.

"Hello, suicide hotline. If this is an emergency, please hang up and call 9-1-1 or go to your nearest emergency room."

It is a repeat caller named Gordon. He is drunk, sitting on a curb.

He tells me how disgusting the world is. How hurt he is, physically and emotionally. He rolled his ankle on the curb. He fell in a puddle. As he talks, he gets up and takes an elevator to the top of a parking garage.

He is almost incoherent.

I ask, "How close are you to the ledge?"

He belches. "Literal one or figurative?" It sounds like *liral* and *firative*.

I say, "Either."

"Pretty close."

"Why don't you step back from that ledge, my friend?"

"You wanna be my friend?"

"Yes, Gordon. I am your friend."

"I probably don't like you very much, then." He snorts. "I'm out with 'the boys' tonight."

"Again?"

"Yeah. You know how my buddy called off his wedding? The one who was always cheating on his fiancée?"

I tell him I recall the boy about whom he is speaking.

"Right. So, we all went out tonight to 'take care' of him. Like he needs it. First he shows up at my place to pregame and gets blitzed on weed and Johnnie Walker. Then I have to listen to him talk about all the bitches we're gonna pull tonight and shit. I guess he's probably going through more than he wants to let on, but still. And I'm just sitting there, thinking about how someone was willing to *marry* this fucking schmuck. Then the rest of the boys come over and we all go out. I spend the night listening to them say stuff like 'Damn, that bitch is built like a brick shithouse.' Stuff like that. And I'm just thinking how we were all supposed to go out for a good time, and they can't think of anything but bitches."

I picture him on top of the garage. Button-down shirt, thin stripes. One of those ball caps with the rigid brim and sticker. Shiny Levi's jeans. Either white sneakers or knockoff loafers.

He tells me he doesn't know how it's possible that he's the one who should feel so alone.

He tells me that he's only even friends with "the boys" because of obligation.

He tells me he's sick to death of always getting dragged along in the tide.

"Gordon," I say. "Would you like to hear a story?"

He burps. I hear bile rise in his throat.

✦ ✦ ✦

I sit with my father's revolver in hand. Rachael has not spoken to me in weeks.

I drink a fifth of blended scotch. I place the revolver against my temporal lobe. I fall asleep crying.

The next day I awake and lock the revolver in a safe in my closet. It is a new day, and although I am not thankful for my life, I am contented to lay on a towel in the sun and pass the day thoughtlessly.

✦ ✦ ✦

Gordon says, "Yeah, and?"

"Think of the joys I would have missed had I not put the gun away—there is no possible way to quantify how valuable each one is. There is an old saying that suicide is a permanent solution to a temporary problem."

"That's fucking stupid. Who doesn't want permanent solutions to things?"

"Your negative feelings will pass with time and help, Gordon. Do not behave rashly."

"Rashly?" He processes the word. "These friends I have, they may not know that they're pieces of shit, but they're happy. Know why? Cause they're out there doing what they want. Being men. Taking action. Maybe I should take some action."

"I do not think you are lacking the tools necessary to self-actualize in a less drastic fashion."

His voice drifts. "Nah. I never had those . . . tools to . . . what you said."

I take a breath to begin talking.

Gordon cuts me off. "I already know what you're gonna say. But if I walk back down . . . it'd just feel like I'm the little kid leaving the line for the high dive, you know? Everyone stares. 'Cause they know I'm a coward. I'm sick of never doing what I want. I'm sick of not having the balls to tell my scumbag buddy he's a piece of shit."

"Gordon, there are right and wrong ways to change. Choose carefully."

He asks, "You ever wonder if the life you lived after you locked up the gun was worth it?"

Every night.

I say, "I know it was worth it." I hear him stumbling around. The air moves around his phone's mouthpiece. "Finding out what is to come is the beauty of living. No longer having those experiences in store for you is the tragedy of death."

"I think you're full of shit," he mumbles.

"Gordon," I say. "Tell me where you are. Exactly. Right now."

"I already told you—" burp, hiccup, vomit, swallow "—I'm at the parking garage by the bar."

I hiss, "What bar?"

His voice changes. "What if you're wrong? About life. About death. About everything."

I bite back anger. The layers weigh heavily. "Gordon," I repeat. "Where *are* you?"

He swallows hard. "I think I'm done."

"Gordon. So help me. Do—not—jump."

"That's my problem. I never jump. Only fall."

I listen hard. My enhanced hearing picks up the sound of a live jazz band. This gives me three options for areas in which Gordon may be. Having lived in the same place for a very long time, you come to know the sounds of neighborhoods like favorite songs. I leave so quickly that I don't hear the headset hit the floor until I am out on the narrow street at the bottom of my hill.

I stop at the first option. No garage near it. I try the next. The crowd is too rowdy; I would have heard them on the phone.

The third option. There is a garage two blocks away.

I reach the garage a moment after Gordon splashes onto the pavement.

Droplets of his blood pepper my face. I roll him over with a toe. He is dressed to my prediction.

White sneakers. Not loafers.

He went down face first, so I cannot tell what he looked like before. A weak breeze brushes my ear as his hat flutters down.

It bears the symbol of a minor-league baseball team. There is no sticker on the brim, but it is utterly clean.

I do not let it touch the ground. I put it on my head, crunching it over dried-out hair, adjusting it over flaking skin.

I walk home, staring at the moon. It is large and dominates the night sky, burning with the reflected fury of the sun. I enter my bedroom. Jerry has eaten all the food and drunk all the water. He sleeps in a fetal ball. I unfold him and chain his arm back to the radiator.

Tonight, I am not hungry.

✦ ✦ ✦

I awaken to the frantic shrill of the phone. It is still daytime, but sleep is no longer an option. I pace back and forth before the door, waiting until I feel the sun set. I would not die if I left my bedroom sooner, but I am, even after all this time, a creature of habit. Each unanswered ring stabs my ears and chills my cold heart. Jerry stirs and curses at me vehemently. I allow it; my mind is on other things.

Finally, it is night.

Rich is my first call.

"Not now," I say.

He answers, "Okay."

This is not common but it happens. Rich is very understanding.

I console a grieving husband. A single mother of two who has reached the height of her stress limit and is holding a prescription bottle of antidepressants in one hand, a scotch in the other. She is on speakerphone because she "just doesn't have the energy to hold the phone or care who hears this shit anymore."

I tell them both that the perceived solution to their problems will just be the cause of more pain for the world. I tell them how strong they are for calling. I tell them I am here whenever they need me. Neither started their calls crying. Both end in tears.

I say, "Please, if you ever need to talk again, call me."

They both say they will. These are the kinds of calls that won't be followed up on for months or years, if ever.

Jacob calls.

"So I guess I have a good memory," he says.

"That must be very helpful for your job."

"Shut up. You know what I'm talking about. That homework shit you gave me. I got to thinking of this ex I dated in college. We were happy, I think—for a bit, anyway. She was a Roman Catholic. Raised real religious in the boonies. And so she didn't ever want to, like, have sex. Or at least that's what she said. I mean, I could have, I think, but she always said it was important for her to wait till marriage or whatever. So I never, like, pressured her about it.

"But anyway, there was this night, after I dropped out but before I reenrolled, where I was visiting, and she wanted us to go to her room, and I knew if we did she'd suck my dick or whatever. We were watching a movie—this was really early in our relationship. Some stupid action movie that you don't really have to pay attention to, and she's like 'Let's go to my room.' And I said I didn't think we should. I told her I just wanted to sit and watch the movie and be with her. It made her so happy she cried. It made me smile, remembering that. Just to know that my actions could make someone so happy they cried."

I tell him that sounds lovely.

He agrees. Then he says, "But it's also really sad if you think further into it, you know? Like the fact that a dude would *just* want to hang out with her was a cause for sheer joy. Because it wasn't all about sex. That's sad. Who teaches kids to think that way? On both sides. I mean, Christ."

He starts crying.

He mumbles, "I just want that feeling back. And I can't find it."

This is something I understand. Happiness is fleeting. In the end, everything is. "Do you talk to this girl any longer?"

"Never. She told me a year or so back that she wants nothing to do with me. It's hard to blame her. All the drunk phone calls. Me complaining, weighing her down. Story of my life."

I ask him if he believes the girl ever looks upon that memory fondly.

"I don't know. Maybe? I haven't tried to talk to her since she said we shouldn't."

"I believe she probably does."

"Why? You've never even fucking met her." His pain turns to anger. "For that matter, you've never even met me. You don't know shit."

Despite feeling that my comment was rather innocuous and his response unwarranted, I choose to let him continue.

He says, "Sometimes I look at pictures of us on the internet. We were really happy once. We were. I know it. But I can't get that back. It's so hard to meet people these days. And everyone wants this crazy, ideal, perfect love."

I tell him when you get older you realize why they call it "settling."

I say, "At your age no one knows what they want. You are between complete hormonal drive and intellectual maturity."

He tells me he bought a gun today, just in case.

I ask what happened to the noose.

"I googled death by asphyxiation. It sounds horrible."

Everyone just wants the miracle cure for pain. There is no such thing. "Any way to die is terrible."

"How . . . uh . . . how did you die?" he asks.

"There are certain moments that are dangerous to relive."

I hear him nod. "Been there."

"Focus on your small joys. Do you have a daily routine?"

"Yeah. But I fucking *hate* it."

"I have advice for you."

"What?"

"Try a new thing. Stick to your routine, and look at your day as just that: a day. If it goes poorly, there will be another tomorrow, if you let there be. But change one thing. Carve out a little piece of time for yourself."

"What would I even try? Video games? I already watch enough Netflix. It's just wasting time."

"Go outdoors. Have you ever thrown a boomerang? Doing it properly can be a very rewarding endeavor."

"A boomerang? Dude, this isn't fucking Australia."

"What does that have to do with anything?"

"Why a boomerang?"

"When I was alive, throwing a boomerang once brought me unexpected good fortune."

"How so?"

✦ ✦ ✦

Twenty-eight. Healthy back. Spry on my feet. A bit uncoordinated, but with enough in the reflex department to get me through my days. There is a park a short walk from my apartment. It is generally vacant during the winter, apart from hunched-up people in coats trying to coax their dogs into going to the bathroom.

I take my boomerang, cock it to my ear, and throw it with some force. It does not exactly come back to me. I pick it up from the frosted grass. I throw it again and again, but it never returns properly. A dog beats me to it on one occasion. I smile at his owner, a blonde girl who smiles back in a dazzling fashion.

"Sorry about him," she says as she wrestles the boomerang from his mouth and hands it to me. It now has small tooth marks on the side.

I tell her it is not a problem. She stands beside me curiously. I move to the side and throw the boomerang. My aim is predictably off. She catches it deftly and hands it back to me.

"Try adjusting your wrist so you throw in a straight line," she advises.

"Like this?"

She shakes her head, moves my hand. "Now try."

The boomerang returns. I fumble it the first time but catch it on the second attempt. The dog chases his tail and falls down. His tongue lolls from the side of his mouth so that he seems to smile.

"Would you like to throw?" I ask.

She nods and takes the boomerang. Her throw is imperfect, but she reaches behind herself to snag it from the air.

I laugh. "I think you may be slightly more athletic than I am."

She says, "Oh, without a doubt."

I ask if she drinks coffee. To my extreme pleasure, she does.

We walk to her apartment. She lives on the second floor of her building. We drop her dog off and then sit down at a corner café. We drink too much coffee and laugh at sarcastic jokes and nonsensical imitations of newspaper articles.

We stay until the sun sets.

She says, "Oh dear, time has gotten away."

She tells me that I have her address now and she is off on Thursdays.

Then she kisses my cheek.

✦ ✦ ✦

I tell Jacob that you often meet the best people under unusual circumstances.

He asks what happened to Rachael. The story I have just told, of course, happened before I met her.

I say, "Your life will not consist of the love of one person. Destiny has a funny way of introducing those who need to meet. So go to a park. Throw a boomerang."

He scoffs and hangs up.

I enter my bedroom. Jerry has freed his hand and whips a dog bowl at me. It catches me on the forehead and bangs off my skull. I stagger. He has managed to undo the chains binding his feet. He slings the chains at me.

I catch the whip of chains and let it coil around my wrist. He snarls and yanks it toward himself. I grip and pull back. The arm chained to the radiator dislocates at the shoulder. Jerry gasps in agony.

Jerry infuriates me. I have had a perfectly acceptable evening to this point. Who is he to try and take that away?

Looking at him reminds me of Margie all alone in that apartment.

Of Rachael's rapist.

I rip his throat out, drinking from the fountain of arterial spray. He dies with a look of startled rage. His blood stains the concrete a dull red that will turn rust brown. I continue to feed even after he collapses, draining all the nourishment I can.

That day, I sleep on blood-soaked sheets.

✦ ✦ ✦

Disposing of a body is surprisingly easy once you have done it a few times. Dumpsters are excellent options. My fingerprints have long since sloughed off, so I do not worry about gloves. Jerry's body thunks into the aluminum rectangle. The plastic lid bangs closed. I wipe my hands in the style of movie mobsters and shove them into pockets with holes in the bottoms.

The city's nightlife, no matter the generation, does not change. Subtle details are different, but the debauchery is identical. This decade demands men in loosely buttoned shirts and ankle boots. Women in short, glimmering dresses, alcohol adding a wobble to their gait. Both parties' hair is clean and styled. Boys and girls sway and stare at cell phones and ask each other for advice about how to meet up with potential sexual partners. Perfumes carry on the air. Artificial laughter rings. Dancing begins on curbs and sidewalks. Mouths open and intertwine. Bodies melt and gyrate.

It does nothing for me.

Phone calls can wait tonight. Gordon's death has irked me. My mind drifts from him to Jacob. Two boys with essentially the same issue and no stress tolerance. Gordon added alcohol to the equation. This was the solving variable for tragedy.

I return to Margie's building. I buzz her apartment directly. There is no answer. I buzz the old woman from days earlier and use the same ploy to gain entrance. I go back to Miss Havisham's apartment, but instead of knocking on her door, I turn to the apartment across the hall.

I knock hard enough to shake the door in its frame. There is a grunt from inside and the door opens on a chain. A boy in his late twenties peers out. He looks at me with one eye, the other hidden behind his door.

He asks, "Who are you?"

He is looking at my chest. I recognize his voice as the one that screamed at Miss Havisham to "shut the fuck up."

"Pleased to make your acquaintance," I say. "Would you mind speaking to me in the hallway for a moment?"

He seems intrigued. He looks me in the eye. His jaw hangs slack. He closes his door to undo the chain and reopens it. He steps out of his apartment and stands before me, shirtless, wearing what appear to be swim trunks, and barefoot. I ask him if he knows the woman across the hall.

He sighs. "Yeah. She's the worst neighbor in the fucking world. I just want her to be quiet at night so I can watch some TV."

Anger rises in my chest. "She is an old woman, with no apparent family. Have you considered this?"

He shrugs. "Not my problem."

"It is now."

He tilts his head. I focus on his eyes. His jaw hangs loose once more.

I tell him he is now responsible for Miss Havisham, that he will check on her once a day. Ask her if she needs errands run. Tend to her when she makes a commotion. I tell him to be a good neighbor, nay, a good human being, and show a bit of respect for someone who is clearly alone and not doing very well.

He nods listlessly.

I say that if he does not care for Miss Havisham for as long as they live across from one another, I will be very displeased. I explain to him what my displeasure will mean for his well-being.

He says he understands. A note of fear creeps into his voice.

I release him from my hypnotic hold.

I say, "Have a lovely night."

He backs into his apartment, slams the door. I hear him redo the chain and flee deeper into his domicile.

✦ ✦ ✦

I do not check on Miss Havisham. Truth be told, I understand the boy's irritation with her.

I head instead to Margie's numberless door. The smells of stale food and marijuana waft out. I knock.

There is no response.

"Margie." I knock harder. "I'm here to help."

No response.

I tell her, "Please invite me in so we may speak in person."

There is a rustling, so quiet as to be nearly imperceptible. Light footsteps follow. The door opens a crack. Ruddy candlelight wavers through.

She hides behind the door, waiting.

"May I come in?" I ask.

She speaks in a whisper. "What if I say no?"

"Then I will stand in the hallway and try to speak with you."

"And if I say yes?"

"I will come in the apartment and try to speak with you."

"Are you here to eat me?"

"No."

"Are you lying?"

"No."

The door creaks halfway open. Margie still does not appear.

She says, "Come in."

An invisible force dissipates before me and I enter. The stained carpet muffles the sound of my footsteps. The candlelight cannot be enough for human eyes to comfortably see by.

There is a couch in the center of the room, ripped at the top. The television is off, which strikes me as odd given that a teenage girl lives here by herself. There is a small kitchenette, separated from the living room by a change in flooring from brown carpet to red tile, and past it a hall that recedes further into the apartment. The home lacks even the ambient glow of digital clocks and the power lights of miscellaneous electronic devices.

The odors are stronger and fouler inside. Margie's blue eyes are bloodshot and hooded. She holds a cross in her left hand, made of pencils hastily bound together with rubber bands, and raises it as she stands up straighter in a show of strength. She is too frail for the gesture to carry much threat.

"Why is your power out?" I ask.

"Stay back," she says, voice aquiver. "Or I'll kill you."

The end of the cross has been sharpened to a graphite point.

Hands behind me, I step back and away from her.

I say, "I am not here to hurt you. Please answer my question."

She sniffs, stiffens her lip. "I couldn't pay the bill."

"I thought your foster father had money above the fridge."

"Right." Her voice hardens. "But someone didn't think to check if that asshole had the mailbox key on him before snatching him." She fixes me with an irritated look. "And the bills were definitely overdue anyway. I would have tried to pay them online, but I don't exactly qualify for credit cards. So no, I can't pay my bill, can't pay my telephone bills, can't pay my automobills."

No matter how righteous you believe it to be, anger breeds oversights.

"What do automobiles have to do with this?"

"No," she says. "Automo*bills*. It's Destiny's Child."

"I see."

I do not see.

She sighs. "No one gets me. I really like late nineties/early millennium shit. Probably I shouldn't, because it's like the only thing Jerry ever plays, so I feel like me liking it is some kind of weird Stockholm Syndrome thing. But anyway I do, so that puts me in a weird spot where no kids my age really have the same references and the people who would get it are, like, inappropriate ages for me to hang out with. So I'm broke with no friends. This is my life now."

"Destiny's Child," I repeat.

She groans.

"Would you like me to call Children's Services for you?"

"Do you have a phone?"

"Not with me."

"That's weird. Are you, like, really old or something?" She sighs. "Whatever. I don't have one either. Oh! Do they still have phone booths? I have—" she pulls a wad of crushed, wrinkled bills from an oversized pocket "—eight bucks."

"Is that a yes?"

"Ugh. No. I'm trying to make a point."

"Which is?"

"That I don't want you to call."

"Okay."

I turn on one heel and pace about the room. Though squalid, the apartment seems as though it could be a comfortable place to live if given an appropriate amount of care.

"Why are you even here?" she asks.

I tell her I feel guilty.

I say that it is my duty as an adult to check on her.

I apologize for acting without fully considering the consequences of what I was doing. It is unlike me.

*Lie*, says Rich's voice in my head.

"Dude," she says, "you don't know a fucking thing about me. I'm better off now. Don't feel guilty."

"You are living in destitution and squalor."

"What?"

I sigh. Children and their brief attention spans are killing the breadth of expression the English language once offered. "This is not good enough for you," I say.

She snaps, "How do you know what's good enough for me?"

"You are a child. It is the community's responsibility to make sure you are adequately provided for."

"It takes a village or some shit?"

I nod. "Well, yes, but not quite. Have you read Dostoyevsky?"

"Who?"

"Fyodor Dostoyevsky. Do they still teach you *Crime and Punishment* in school?"

"Is that, like, the one where the guy kills that old lady with an axe?"

I nod.

"Oh. Yeah. But I only read the first twenty pages or so. It was great at first, when the old lady gets her head split. After that it was just some sickly dude sitting around bitching. I got bored."

"Fine. Point taken. However, would you consider the title of the book for me?"

She gives me a blank look.

"You have committed no crime to merit this punishment. You are, in a way, the antithesis of Dostoyevsky's tragic protagonist."

She frowns, still wielding her cross. "Just tell me what the fuck you're doing here or get out. I'm tired."

"May I tell you a story?"

✦ ✦ ✦

I am fourteen. My father's home is a two-room apartment on the northeast side of town. There is his bedroom and a living room with alcoves for the stove and exposed toilet. I sleep on a moldy couch, choosing its ragged cushions over the unforgiving metal bars that jut from the foldout bed.

It is late at night and I am supposed to be sleeping. I have an English exam in the morning. My marks in school are fine, but I am nervous about this one. Something crashes in the hall outside. The door begins to rattle, then slams open. There is already a hole in the wall behind it where the knob hits.

My father staggers into the room. He has been sober for the last three days, which is a good stretch for him. He is not sober now. He may have won or lost gambling tonight; it is not particularly important to me which it was. He leans over the couch. His breath is hot by my ear.

"You little bag of shit," he whispers. "All you do is take up space. Space and money. Two things we never have enough of." He stomps through the room, opens the refrigerator. I crack an eyelid. He opens a container and sniffs it, tosses it to the side of the room. His beard is ragged, hat askew.

I quietly stand. I ask, "Are you hungry?"

As he staggers away from the fridge I move past him to the cabinets. There is peanut butter and rye bread. I clean a butter knife lying dirty in the sink.

He tells me it's an embarrassment to see me doing the work of women.

I say nothing.

He says, "This is the work a wife does." Then, louder, "It's what your mother would do, if she was here. If you hadn't killed her."

I make my father's sandwich.

He demands I bring him something to drink. He seems to have forgotten the unlabeled bottle of amber liquid in his hand.

I say, "It seems you already have a drink, Father."

He rips the sandwich from its plate, sending the dish to shatter on the floor. He tells me he's almost done with his bottle, that

I should go get some liquor if I want to continue living beneath his roof.

I do not look him in the eye when I say it is too late at night. I do not bother mentioning that I am too young. He sits down on the couch that is my bed. He smells the sandwich. He says it smells like mustard, despite the impossibility.

He tells me that since the trenches of the war, everything smells like mustard.

He tells me, as he does every night, about when his best friend Ralph clawed himself to death because of the mustard gas.

I make no comment.

"I lose Ralph in a shit-filled trench and then my son rips my wife apart. You—" he points at me with the butt of his bottle "—took the only thing I had left."

He lurches up and swings the bottle wildly at my head.

I step back. He stumbles. I catch him so he does not fall. He shoves me away.

He tells me he doesn't need my help.

He throws the bottle. I do not have to move as it sails widely to the right.

He begins crying.

I lay him gently on the couch.

He catches me around the throat and squeezes until red and green spots swim behind my eyelids. I grip his wrist to wrench it away, clawing at the veined flesh. He shoves me away. I fall against the wall. He is unconscious by the time my bottom hits the floor.

There is a wooden block full of sharpened knives by the stove. I stare longingly at it.

✦ ✦ ✦

Margie asks, "So?"

"My father was not a good man, but he had his own sad past with which to grapple—as does everyone, to varying degrees."

"Jerry was an asshole."

"Undoubtedly so. How are you feeling?"

She shrugs. "I'm pretty high. That feels nice. Before, if Jerry even thought I'd been sniffing around his weed, he'd beat or rape me."

Her inflection does not change at all. There is no hint of sadness in her voice. But it is stamped behind her glassy blue eyes.

I turn my back so I do not have to see those eyes. "You cannot live this way."

"That's how I felt before. Then you took care of that sack of shit."

I turn to face her again. "You need to let me call someone who can properly help you."

"No. They're the people who stuck me here in the first place."

"Fine." I knew it was likely to come to this. "Then you are coming home with me."

She looks dumbstruck. "Dude, you think I'm better off being eaten?"

"I do not wish to eat you."

She points at me. "Vampire." Then at herself. "Human. Isn't that, like, what you guys do?"

"Are there foods you do not like?"

"Eggs."

"Consider sixteen-year-old girls with attitude problems my eggs."

She crosses her arms. "Fuck you, bro."

I frown. "My appetites do not swing that way for sixteen-year-old girls either."

She snorts. "Yeah. I noticed you're not exactly hot or anything. Not like how they show vampires on TV."

"Maintaining a glamour takes a considerable amount of energy—energy that I need to preserve in order to convince *children* not to kill themselves. Whether they intend to do so directly or by refusing freely offered help."

"Do me a fucking favor and put one up. You're making me nauseous."

I bare my fangs and hiss. She raises a skeptical eyebrow. Muttering about who makes whom nauseous and her current hygienic state, I wave a hand. Margie's eyes grow large.

"Wow," she says. "You're totally hot. Do you fuck people looking like that?"

"I am not interested in sex."

"I thought that was the other thing you guys liked. Blood and sex."

"We have already had this conversation. However, I have considered this facet of popular culture, and I believe that the lore surrounding vampires and sex is rather logical. Sexual arousal increases heart rate and blood flow. Engaging in it might, under some circumstances, make feeding easier. Think of it as increasing the water pressure in a fountain."

"But you don't wanna fuck things."

"Child, I am dead. Most of my surface receptors have decayed past functionality."

Her lips screw into a grimace. "Yeah. That makes sense. Well, apart from the hotness thing, are you closer to Dracula or Edward Cullen?"

"Edward Cullen?"

"Yeah. The *Twilight* vampire? The cheesy, shitty one that falls in love with the boring average girl for, like, no reason? They have this weird possessive relationship and it's kind of Mormon but not really. Oh, and the vampires, like, glitter in the sun and play baseball."

"Not that one."

"So, Dracula?"

"I suppose that is closer, in fact."

"So you get hungry and you kill people."

"Occasionally. Yes. I try to kill only those who hurt others."

"Like Dexter?"

I sigh. "These references seem to be lost on me. Who is Dexter?"

"From TV, you know? The serial killer that only kills bad guys."

"What makes them bad?"

"You know. Bad. Bad people. Like, they commit crimes. Murderers and pedophiles and shit."

"That does seem rather bad."

"Yeah, but *bad* is a pretty relative term, though. So there are varying levels of it, right? Like, how bad does someone have to be for you to eat them?"

For whatever reason, I do not explain that bad people are the ones who intentionally hurt others. Instead I say, "Bad people are like pornography. I know them when I see them."

She gives me a blank look. "So, this whole suicide hotline thing, it's not about finding people to eat?"

I frown. "Can you elaborate?"

"I was just thinking that maybe you use this hotline to identify, like, victims. Then come and eat them. You know, like a predator."

"That is an interesting thought," I tell her. "I had not considered that, nor do I wish to hurt those in need of help. I am not here to kill or eat you. I wish to improve your quality of life from this . . . distasteful ruination."

She is silent for a long time, looking at my forehead.

I understand her hesitancy to look me in the eye. Eye contact is often dangerous—with anyone. You may learn more than you wanted to know.

She says, "Promise that you won't just fucking kill me."

"I promise."

A promise, especially today, may not seem like much. But keeping one's word is important. You learn this as you grow older. You see more of the damage caused by a broken promise the longer you have to observe its effects.

"So, that's, like, binding on you, right? Because of the whole supernatural angle. You can't break a promise. Right?"

I tell her that's true.

She asks, "Did you kill Jerry?"

Yes.

"No."

"Why not?"

"I wasn't hungry. The unnecessary taking of life is the greatest sin, even for the undead. When I need to feed—think of it like hunting, but not for sport. For survival."

"Hunting is still wrong."

"For sport, yes, I agree. As would Kant. However, survival is important. It preserves your ability to affect the world in a positive manner."

She mutters that I sound like a basic bitch misquoting Gandhi. "So killing is the greatest sin. But you occasionally kill people."

My lips purse. "I suppose a certain degree of hypocrisy is inevitable when you have lived as long as I."

She shakes her head. "Then how could I possibly trust you?"

This is a fair question. "I suppose that is the decision you must make. Whether or not to trust me. That said, keep in mind that I have so far engaged in no ill treatment of you, nor shown any intention to do so."

"Yeah, but this could just be an elaborate ploy to get me to your lair or whatever. Without a struggle."

I want to tell her that if I wished to take her by force, struggling would be of no use. Instead I say, "I have no desire to take you anywhere against your will. Say the word and I will depart willingly."

She is quiet for a full minute as she contemplates this. "Say I do leave with you. Are there gonna be, like, rotting corpses and stuff? People you plan on eating?"

"No. In this day and age, there are very easy alternatives to killing in order to obtain blood. Consider me, for all intents and purposes, nothing more than a human being with extra living space in which you can stay."

"All right. Yeah. I'll go. For a few days—as a trial or whatever. *If* I can bail at any point in time and you won't try to stop me or, like, pursue me."

"I consent to these terms."

"Okay."

"Good." I sniff the air. "Your odor tells me the water is out as well. You will shower. And then we will find you provisions before daylight."

"Do you have money? I'm pretty much out."

I smile. She shrinks away.

✦ ✦ ✦

Margie cranes her neck. "Whoa. This is your house?"

"Yes."

"Holy shit. You're fucking *loaded.* Guess I didn't need to ask about money."

I do not answer but proceed up the hill.

My home is a Tudor mansion, occupying the entirety of a

hilltop that was leveled off when it was built. It is no longer in the best condition, with vines crawling up the walls and browned grass growing long and sideways all around it. Gnarled trees bow away from the house. All living things fear the dead, if only because they fear the inevitable. There are beer cans scattered on the ground. To my knowledge, the children who come to the surrounding area to drink, smoke marijuana, and fornicate do not enter my home.

It is known the house is inhabited, that the owner does not welcome guests, and (after several break-ins a few years ago) that entering the house uninvited can do funny things to a person's mind. There is, of course, no way to prove this.

I push the doors open for Margie. They creak loudly. Margie comments that if she were in a horror movie, that would have been so totally predictable. Then she lets out a low whistle. The house is lit by the bright moon shining through French windows above the doors. A grand mahogany staircase runs up from the foyer. To our left is a dining room, with a long walnut table beneath an iron chandelier. The chairs are also walnut, upholstered with red cushions. The sitting room to our right has a large bay window at the front, which lets the moonlight pool on a velvet Victorian sofa. Everything is elegant. Everything has a greyish tint from layers of dust.

I lead Margie up the stairs, half-listening to her torrent of sarcastic comments that occasionally seem to be compliments. I show her the master bedroom, a lavish affair with a canopied four-poster bed, dresser, vanity, and armoire. There is a bathroom en suite, tiled in marble. The toilet is stained with rust but functional. The windows in this room are smaller and the moon does not provide adequate illumination. Margie flicks a light switch on the wall. Nothing happens; the bulbs in the ceiling need replacing. I light a lantern and lower the shutter so as to not shock Margie's eyes.

Her face lights with more than the lantern's glow.

"Holy fucking mother of shit," she exclaims.

I cannot conceal my pleasure at hers.

She says, "I mean it's, like, totally fucking filthy, and the colors are awful, but holy shit."

The room is decorated in shades of burgundy and red.

"What is wrong with the colors?"

She snorts. "Men."

"This is where you will stay. Unless one of the other rooms pleases your aesthetic more."

"No. This is fucking awesome."

She runs and jumps on the bed, bouncing.

"Do not jump on the bed."

"Whatever, *Dad*."

"This room suits you, then?"

"Uh, yeah."

"Cool."

"Cool?"

"Cool."

"Okay," she says. "Questions."

"Yes?"

"Is there wi-fi?"

"Internet?"

"Wireless internet."

"No."

She scowls. "Can I have a cell phone?"

"No."

"Why not?"

"Do you have one currently?"

"No. But all the girls at school do. I want one."

"No."

She pouts and crosses her arms. It is a familiar posture. Something gives way in me.

I tell her we can discuss it further at a later date.

"Fine. But I need the internet. For, like, school and stuff."

"There is a computer downstairs."

"Wait—there's a downstairs, too?"

"That is where I live."

She snorts. "Typical vampire."

"Would you like to see it?"

She does not find it necessary to answer, only grabs the lantern and strides into the hallway. She explores the second floor a bit more. I glide behind her.

"What's this locked room?"

"If you wish to stay here you will leave that room alone."

"Spoopy." Her gaze lingers on the door until I clear my throat and motion her towards the staircase. "What's in there that you don't want me to see?"

"Do not concern yourself with that. I wish for that space to remain private. You will need to respect that wish."

Beneath the grand entrance staircase is my door. It is camouflaged, with a circular knob set back into the wood. I open it and we step into a spiral staircase. Sconces on the walls bathe it in a moody half-light.

"You are such a cliché," Margie says.

"Clichés become clichés for a reason."

"Whatever, Mister I-Rationalize-All-My-Behaviors."

"You are a bit too perceptive for your own good."

We emerge into the main basement. A throw rug sewn with a depiction of Rembrandt's *The Night Watch* cozies the concrete floor. A tall bookcase overflows with my favorite works of fiction—if you can call them that. I have always found that excellent fiction can provide more information about the human condition than a great multitude of statistics.

Numbers never lie, but they will say whatever you please.

I fold up the throw rug to reveal a trap door of thick maple, reinforced several times. Margie takes the ring and tugs to no avail.

She says, "Holy hell, man." (It is always nice to hear that some still consider me human.) "That's really fucking heavy."

I twist my mouth in distaste.

I tell her I would much prefer it if she could attempt to swear less.

She tells me to shove it in a choice area of my body that I do not think I would enjoy.

It is difficult not to be charmed by her spirit and ferocity.

A strong grip and pull opens the door. An old ladder runs down into the darkness. Margie leaves the lantern behind to climb onto the ladder. I follow. The door slams shut behind us.

There are no lights.

Margie asks how much further.

"Not far."

"Seriously, dude, how long? I'm tired."

Her feet touch the floor. The power lights of the phone and computer glow from deeper within the room.

"I can't see," Margie says. Her voice quavers slightly.

I do not tell her that's for the best, though she seems to sense it. Instead, I go to the computer and move the mouse. The screen is blinding in the dark room. Margie shields her eyes and hugs herself.

"It's so cold down here. What the hell?" She looks over at me. She is terrified. The initial excitement of exploring the house is gone.

The reality of the situation finally dawns on me.

"Stay put," I tell her. I retrieve a woolen blanket from upstairs and return.

Margie drapes the blanket about herself and grips it tight at the front, keeping it closed. This seems to reassure her. She turns a slow circle. There is still a note of fear when she mockingly imitates my voice. "How very dreary."

I stick my tongue out at her and blow a raspberry.

She snorts. "Look at that. You do have a personality."

I do not show her the room in which I sleep. Where her foster father's blood once soaked into the floor.

I say, "You may use the computer at night, when I am awake. We will go and get you any other things you need. You will have to tell me what those are, of course."

"That's it?"

"Other rules will be made as they show themselves to be necessary."

She opens her mouth to speak.

"No cell phone," I say.

"Ugh. Warm clothes would be a start."

I sniff the air. "Soap would be a start."

She blows a raspberry at me. I pretend not to notice when she discreetly sniffs her armpit and her face falls.

I ask Margie if she would like to use the upstairs bathroom where there is a hot shower.

I say that I do in fact have a water heater and to please stop complaining.

I answer that I can open the door for her.

✦ ✦ ✦

Margie showers for close to an hour. When she is finished there are only a few hours until sunrise. She is visibly tired when she emerges from the bathroom, wearing the same ratty clothing as before.

I tell her we are going to the twenty-four-hour superstore.

She says that's miles away.

She says she's tired.

She says she's fine for now.

"What if I told you we would travel in style?"

"I'd almost believe you, because of the mansion, but then I wouldn't, because it's broken-down and dirty as fuck."

"Consider this a different kind of style. Better than a limousine and without having to spend a single dime."

"What?"

I open the large French windows. My bones crack and shift. If I could still feel pain, this process would certainly be excruciating. Margie, her composure restored by the fact that I have not yet attempted to eat her, observes with academic curiosity.

"Cool," she says.

I wonder how young she was when she started to emotionally disengage like this. It is concerning.

Flapping enormous, leathery wings, I rise above her and squeak. She stretches her arms out and I gently wrap my claws all the way around her scarred biceps.

She says, "So the whole bat thing is real, then."

I squeak the affirmative. Some things exist solely because they are fun.

"A lot bigger than I'd have expected."

We lift off and flutter through the open windows.

Margie oohs and ahhs over the circus lights of the city below. The center of the city—as city centers always do—rises high above the outskirts, brighter and taller and richer than the surrounding areas. I take us by the scenic route, banking around glassy skyscrapers, trying to offer Margie views that will introduce a modicum of joy into a life that has thus far been a bleak affair.

The superstore is situated in a neighborhood poorer than Margie's and comparable in many ways to old Jewish ghettos. We land in a dark alley alongside the store. My body cracks back into its human shape.

I take a cart and ignore the inattentive greeter as we enter. The store has linoleum flooring, white speckled with blue and green in irregular patterns. It is dirty and worn. A man is cleaning it on a riding waxer, which seems like a futile endeavor given the size of the crowd traipsing across it even at the witching hour.

I tell Margie to find food. Warm clothes. Something to do for fun that does not involve a screen. She takes the cart and heads straight for the clothing section.

"This stuff is all so fucking cheap," she exclaims. "I could get, like, everything." Her voice trails off. "Or do we have a budget?"

"Get what you'd like." I almost add *within reason* but, on second thought, do not bother.

She asks me repeatedly if her choices are cute, only to contradict my opinions and tell me I have a terrible eye. She picks mostly neutral colors. I suggest something with a bit more vibrancy, offering a fresh-looking summer dress with a tropical sort of print that makes me think of sunlight.

"That's genuinely horrible," she says.

"I do not agree. And it would do wonders to bring out your eyes."

She holds it in front of her and looks in the mirror. The corners of her mouth twitch up. With a sound of disgust, she throws the dress in the cart. I do not gloat; this would be rude. The rest of the cart is full of men's flannels, skinny jeans, cloth sneakers, UGG boots, graphic tees, pajama pants, and tights.

"Where will you put the food?" I ask.

"We'll get a new cart."

She half-walks with noticeable pep to a register where a bored cashier leans on her elbows.

Margie smiles as she leaves the clothing with the obviously annoyed cashier, whom she quietly calls a bitch as we retrieve our second cart.

Next, my new charge heads for the snack aisle. She fills the cart with chips in colorful plastic bags and cookies in bright boxes.

I say that I told her to buy food.

She ignores me.

With a sigh, I go and collect items with vitamin content: frozen vegetables, apples and bananas, chicken and steaks, peanut butter, rice. I add a gallon of whole milk because her paleness speaks of a significant vitamin D deficiency.

I add these things to the cart as she plunders the aisles of junk food.

I ask, "Do you know how to cook?"

She shrugs. "I wasn't, like, planning on it, but if I have to, I guess. You have a computer. Google has recipes. How hard can it be?"

I realize just how much the girl has to learn.

When we come to the toiletries, she picks out a toothbrush but overlooks paste. I correct the oversight discreetly. She chooses industrial-sized bottles of shampoo, conditioner, and some sort of gel soap. I tell her to get a loofah or washcloth. She asks what for and I explain the concept of exfoliation.

"Ugh. No. I think I'll just use my hands."

"You need something with texture to exfoliate your skin, young lady. Texture."

She grabs a pack of disposable razors. I catch her by the wrist. She rolls her eyes and tells me she needs to shave her legs and pussy, the latter being a word I find more distasteful than most.

"I do not like the idea of you having access to razors. Especially during the day when I am asleep."

She snorts. "Who the fuck tries to kill themselves during the day?"

I frown.

She tells me she is also buying scissors to make her jeans acceptable, and that I need to get over it.

"What about entertainment?" I ask.

"You have a computer."

I do not press the issue. We approach the register where the cart of clothing waits. The cashier yawns. She scans items and tosses them helter-skelter into plastic bags attached to a rotating metal rack, removing security tags as she goes. Margie collects the bags as they fill, placing them in our carts.

The cashier reads off the total dollar amount, assigning a concrete value to Margie's new life. Margie seems to find the number both pleasant and appalling. I believe the discomfort is mostly for show.

The cashier's eyes meet mine. Her jaw goes slack and she nods when I tell her to please void the transaction. As she thanks us for our patronage, Margie looks up at me questioningly. I shrug and explain that this is simply capitalism at work. Margie grabs one cart and pushes it towards the doors. The greeter stops us to check our receipt and receives the same treatment as the cashier. We pass unmolested.

Margie and I stand outside in the crisp air. I breathe deeply. It has been a long time since I've had a reason to be out so close to morning. The scent of baked goods creeps into the air. Fog begins to lift in the warmth of the approaching dawn. Time is running short.

I tell Margie to wait here and I bend the sides of the carts to create rounded cages. Hoisting one cart onto each shoulder, I break into my fastest run and am home within minutes. The cart with the clothing goes in Margie's room and the one with the food in the kitchen. I return for Margie. She is listing, mostly asleep, against the store's wall.

Dawn's ambient light greys and purples the sky. We move to the alley for privacy, and when I have changed we fly away, my wings beating hard to race the sun. We glide through the window just in time and I release her to land with a small thud on the floor.

"Put your clothing away in your room and the food in the pantry," I say, and then I am gone to my subbasement and safety.

Jerry's blood has been bleached away, but I can still smell it in the pores of the concrete.

# Chapter Three

I rise when it is night again, shoulders and knees creaking as I climb the ladder rungs. Margie is in the kitchen. Empty packages of junk food are scattered across the counters. Her fingers are grubby with artificial cheese.

"Morning, Sunshine," she says.

She is wearing the blue sundress. It does, in fact, do wonders for her eyes.

"How are you feeling?" I ask.

"Full. Bored. Do you have any booze in this place?"

"No. Drinking is bad for depression. And you are underage. We will not be acquiring any."

"Whatever. Can I get on the computer already?"

"Did you attend school today?"

She laughs. "Nah."

"Tomorrow, you will."

"Um, excuse me, *Dad.* I don't think so."

"Then you are no longer welcome here."

I turn on my heel and head towards the basement.

Margie charges up and grabs my wrist.

"Hold on, hold on, hold on. Where the fuck will I go?"

"You will go to school."

"But there's no bus stop around here, and I can't drive. We're pretty fucking far away from my school, you know. And given that it happens during the day, I don't think *you* could exactly get me there."

"Do you have a friend who could drive you?"

She hugs herself. I cannot tell if her distress is genuine.

"I don't really have any friends. No one wants to talk to the emo girl with the scars on her arms who spends half the day with the guidance counselor. But whatever. I don't like talking to people anyway."

"What if I make arrangements for a car to pick you up each morning and bring you back each afternoon?"

"Seriously?"

"Yes. I am serious."

"Okay. Okay, yeah, I could do that."

"Excellent. You may follow me and use the computer."

She starts. I ask her what she's forgetting.

"Oh, right."

She runs upstairs and comes back in a down-stuffed jacket, flannel pajama pants with sweats over them, and a pair of her UGG boots. She rams a wool cap down over her ears and snaps off a salute to me.

"Margot Bishop, winter warrior, at your service."

"Margot?"

"Yeah. That's my full name or whatever. It's lame, but I tell myself I'm named for that Wes Anderson movie where Gwyneth Paltrow is a total mess but somehow a total inspiration at the same time. It used to play on Comedy Central all the time in the mornings? You have no idea what I'm talking about." She sighs. "You're annoying."

I tilt my head. "I have not seen this film."

"No shit. Whatever, I'll download it on your computer. You'll like it."

"If you say so. Now come. I have missed a full night. There will be calls."

✦ ✦ ✦

I sit at my desk and put on my headset. She boots up the computer.

She asks why I wear "that stupid flat-brim."

"It is called style."

"Dude. You really need, like, a fucking *Vogue* or something."

Her focus reverts to the computer, where her eyes glaze as she settles in, clicking and typing away.

The phone rings.

"I tried calling you last night," Jacob says.

I tell him, "I am sorry. I had matters which required my attention."

"Whatever. I'm mostly just calling to tell you I think you're a fucking idiot anyway."

"That is not very nice."

"Neither is telling someone that throwing a fucking *boomerang* will make them feel better."

"The boomerang was not the point. You are dissatisfied with the current state of your life. Try new things."

He says, "I hit some guy in the back because I didn't know what the fuck I was doing. He was pissed. I thought he was gonna kick my ass."

"Did he?" I ask.

"No."

"Well, all right then. How are you feeling otherwise?"

"Like shit."

"Elaborate, if you will."

"I wrote this article for work. Put a lot of time and effort into it. I was proud of it and whatnot. Sent it to my boss and he basically told me to go fuck myself. I'm pretty sure I'm just a total fucking failure, you know? I'm bad at sports. I'm bad at my job. No girl I feel any interest in is even vaguely interested in me. It's just such a fruitless grind."

At least he is not crying this time. Although an incipient apathy can be just as dangerous. When the emotions inevitably return, they can be entirely overwhelming.

"You are not a failure, Jacob—"

"And how the fuck would you know that? Jesus Christ. Why do I keep calling you?"

"You would have to answer that. I am here to listen."

"Listen to this: I hate myself. I really do. I work in advertising, for God's sake. What do I contribute to the world? Nothing. I find new and interesting ways to lie to people to get them to buy shit they don't need."

"What does anyone need?" I ask. "Food. Shelter."

His voice quiets. "Love."

"Yes. That is nice, but it is something that comes when destiny deems it appropriate."

"You're about to tell me a fucking story, aren't you?"

"Yes."

✦ ✦ ✦

Jeanine, the blonde from the park, meets me at the corner of her apartment building. It is a comfortable evening. She wears a long red dress and a shawl drapes her shoulders. Her hair is in intricate braids, pinned high on her head. She smiles and the temperature of the air goes up. I tug on my collar and smile back.

She tells me not to look so uptight. We're going to have fun.

I have not yet told her that I am not a skilled dancer.

She aptly guesses that I am not a skilled dancer.

We walk side by side, occasionally bumping shoulders and stepping lightly away. The dance club is several blocks away, where the housing prices increase and the nighttime lighting brightens. Jeanine and I arrive at a single wooden door with no sign. A top-heavy man sits on a stool outside with crossed arms. He looks Jeanine up and down indecently. His eye twinkles.

"Nice pull," he says, motioning us through the door.

Jeanine nudges me in the ribs. "It's a compliment," she says. "I'm very attractive."

Horns blare from a stage in the corner of the wooden room. Tables are scattered throughout the room and people are dancing around and between them, all dressed to the proverbial nines. Jeanine grips my chin, kisses my mouth, and twirls into the fray.

I watch for a time. Her features are not what one would call classically beautiful. There is a charming asymmetry that does not grace the faces of models, an angular quality subtly sharper at the cheeks. Her ears are small, eyes alight.

She is the most stunning woman in the room.

The men take notice. Many of their dance partners glare.

Appraising the crowd, I think that every woman in this bar is beautiful in her own right. However, Jeanine is a creature of a different order. I watch Jeanine's watchers and feel inadequate.

She spins back to me, takes my wrists in her hands.

She says that she's good enough to make it look like I'm the one leading. That I shouldn't worry.

We move out onto the floor. Our hands intertwine. She takes me between tables and into sparse openings amid the crowd. I am dizzy with motion and euphoria. We arrive at the bar, panting and laughing. She orders a vodka soda. I order ginger ale and whistle along to a softer tune that comes on.

She tells me that whistling is a talent. She tells me I am talented.

I fall in love with her then.

✦ ✦ ✦

"Well, fucking bully for you, man."

"My point is that love can strike in odd places."

"That's not an *odd* place. That's some straight-up, pseudorealist-romantic-comedy bullshit."

"At the time it was odd. Those places were havens of debauchery. Love was rarely involved."

"Wow, you went to a club. How exciting."

"Sarcasm hurts."

He grumbles, "Look, all I'm saying is that times aren't what they were. Meeting people doesn't just happen anymore. The internet and everything . . . it's so hard to just have a conversation. I've tried talking to girls at bars and stuff. But I really don't want to be a creep. So then there's all this pressure and I panic. Then, when I do get the courage to talk, I'm not really in it and they can totally tell. Then I fail and flounder and feel like a floundering failure. You know?"

"Son, listen—"

"Son?"

"I have been feeling vaguely paternal these past few days. Do not ruin it for me. The internet opens avenues of communication. It does not shut them. If you think your interpersonal skills are lacking, practice them. That is why they are called skills. Some people have more natural talent than others, but if you do not work on them they will never improve."

He says, "But if I have this crippling fear of even making eye contact with strangers, how can I practice?"

"Just do it."

"I don't want to."

"Then stop whining."

"Then I'll kill myself."

I pause for a moment. "Was that a joke?"

He laughs long and hard.

I tell him this was *not* funny.

"I don't know," he says. "I got a good laugh from it."

I repeat myself.

He sighs. "What exactly do you want me to do?"

"Talk to a stranger."

"Were you not listening? I don't know how."

"Is the weather supposed to be nice this week?"

"Hold on, let me check. Ugh, this fucking app is so spotty." He clicks his tongue. "Finally. Um, yeah, tomorrow, actually."

"Do you work?"

"Unfortunately."

"When you leave work, go lie on a blanket in the grass. Watch the clouds. Relax. There will be other people out if it is nice. Rest. Then, once you are not so anxious, go up to a person, any person at all. Ask if you can sit with them and then ask how their day is going. If what you say is true about the lack of personal interaction these days, someone will be starved for human contact. See how it goes. If it is not a fruitful interaction, do not be discouraged. Try and try again, as they say."

"Your homework sucks huge horse cocks."

He hangs up.

Margot has been glancing up with mild interest throughout

the phone call.

"What happened with Jeanine?" she asks.

I answer the next call.

✦ ✦ ✦

Rich has had an incident with an orderly. He headbutted the orderly in the face. It was because I did not answer my phone. Rich's phone time ran out, and the orderly tried to enforce the rules.

I say hello.

Rich asks where I was.

He says, "I called eight times. Had to restrain me to get the bandages on my head. I needed to talk to you. I haven't been able to talk to anyone but me. I hate me."

I tell him there's nothing hateful about him.

"Liar," he says. "Keep your phone plugged in. When it's connected, you might still be there."

"But when it is disconnected you know I am not."

"*Exactly*," he hisses.

I tell him that he does not own me and I can do what I want.

I tell him I make my own decisions.

I tell him about the call with Jacob and that I think I actually might have the chance to help someone for once.

He tells me the same things he always does. He grumbles about the restraints he was forced to wear.

He tells me he's tired but at least he's not homeless.

"They'll transfer me somewhere."

"Where?"

"Somewhere with one call a month."

"How would you handle that?"

"Bad."

"Shall I intervene?"

"No. Last time was bad."

"It could have been worse," I say.

Lie.

"They mistreated you," I say.

Truth.

"They probably deserved it," I say.

Lie.

"I can't just sit here," I say.

Lie. Lie. Lie.

"That's not a lie," I say.

Rich tells me he wants to say something.

I say, "Fine."

"You'll never grow any if you keep it up. The lying is bad."

"I cannot grow. I am dead."

"A life is a terrible thing to waste."

"I am not alive." Lie. "I died, Rich. Badly. You remember how?"

"Yes. And then you got a second chance."

"As a monster."

"We're all monsters."

His phone time runs out.

"How'd you die?" Margot asks. When I do not answer, she complains, "It smells bad down here. You have any Glade or Lysol or anything in this hole?"

My cleaning of Jerry's blood has apparently failed to stanch the smell of death.

Margot tells me she has downloaded a bunch of songs and that movie, which I should watch if I get bored. She says she's going to bed.

I tell her a car will be at the house for her tomorrow at 6:50 a.m. sharp. She looks at me sideways and says good night.

I receive no more calls that evening. Whether this is good or bad news, in this line of work, you can never be sure.

Margot leaves the trapdoor open. I want to climb up and close it, but refrain.

✦ ✦ ✦

Margot is already on the computer when I emerge from my room the following evening. She giggles at someone who is shouting in an angry voice.

I watch over her shoulder for several minutes. "What is this drivel?"

"*Clueless*. It's a fucking classic. It's on TV all the time. How have you not seen this?"

Standing with my hands behind my back, I watch as one character tells another that she is a virgin who cannot drive. It seems mean-spirited.

Margot summarizes the plot of the film for me.

"That is *Emma* by Jane Austen."

She takes a cigarette from a crumpled yellow pack. I absently pluck it from her hand with thumb and forefinger. She is unperturbed.

"Huh?" she says.

"The story you just described. It is a story by a woman named Jane Austen."

"So what?"

"There is nothing new under the sun."

"You're boring. This is creative. A change of setting changes a story." She redirects her attention to the screen.

I smile. "Well put. How many times have you seen this particular film?"

"Not as many as I'd fucking like."

She returns to ignoring me.

I climb the ladder and confront my bookshelf. A worn copy of *Emma* sits in the topmost right corner, sandwiched between Bronte and Wharton.

*Emma* drops onto the desk in front of Margot.

"You will read this," I tell her.

She skims the book jacket, then hands it back to me.

"No thanks. Sounds lame as fuck."

I push a button and the computer screen goes black.

She asks, "What the shit, man?"

"You may use the computer when you finish reading."

"The light down here sucks. I'll strain my eyes or whatever."

"Staring at that screen does you no better. Come."

She grunts and follows me upstairs. The French windows are still open. I jump to close them. Margot mutters that I'm a control-freak psycho showoff.

We go to the kitchen.

The refrigerator is full of food from the superstore. The freezer has plastic containers of human blood. I take out one of the latter and work the contents into a pan with a spatula. Margot observes silently. She sheds her basement clothes to reveal tattered jeans and an oversized flannel shirt with the sleeves cut off at the elbow.

"Are those the new clothes we just got?" I ask, aghast.

"What? They look good now."

"Did you . . . pour bleach over those jeans?"

"Yes."

"From my closet?"

"Yeah. Why do you have so much of that stuff?"

I turn the flame of the stove down low to allow the blood to simmer gently. Then I change the subject. "Have you eaten a real meal yet or just more garbage food?"

"Food is food, bro."

"Margot—"

Her face darkens. "No one, and I do mean *no one*, calls me Margot. Margie. My name is Margie."

"Margie. Would you be so kind as to allow me to cook dinner for you? It has been a very long time since I have enjoyed food and I would like some vicarious pleasure."

She points to the pan. "Is that an ingredient?"

"No. That is my dinner."

"Where'd the blood come from?"

"A corpse."

"How ominous of you."

I run my tongue over one fang and change my voice to a movie version of a Transylvanian accent. "I vill suck your blooooood."

"Never. Ever. Do that again. It was—" she shifts her voice to that of a Victorian woman "—positively dreadful."

I check the blood with a thermometer. It is 98.6 degrees Fahrenheit. I pour the blood into a mug and sip it.

Margot says, "All right, make my dinner then, woman."

I begin taking ingredients out. "Do you have any aversion to cheese?"

"Um, no. Who doesn't like cheese?"

"Gnocchi?"

"My favorite."

Gorgonzola?

She seems unsure what this is but nods anyway.

Ham?

She's not, like, fucking kosher or whatever.

Chicken?

Dude, just make the food already.

I tell her to stand up and come learn something.

She says, "Nah, I'm gonna read this old shitty book so I can get back on the computer."

I concede.

Begin by preheating the oven to 350 degrees. Sear and then bake the chicken in a cast-iron skillet. Boil water. Cut your ham steak into cubes. Make a roux from flour and butter, then add whole milk and gorgonzola and cheddar cheeses. Boil the gnocchi in the water with a pinch of kosher salt. Stir the cheese sauce until smooth. Fry the ham. Remove the chicken from the oven and allow it to cool. Drain the gnocchi in a colander and then dump it into a glass casserole dish. Pour the ham into the cheese sauce and stir; pour this over the gnocchi. Julienne the chicken and layer across the top. Top with breadcrumbs. Bake for 35 minutes.

I sip blood while cooking.

I have nice china and faux-silver utensils in a cabinet and drawer, respectively. When I am finished with everything, the dish is plated appealingly, with extra cheese sauce spread in a zigzagging pattern beneath the main course. Margot stares.

"That actually smells really good."

I drape a napkin over my forearm and serve her. "Your gnocchi gorgonzola, milady."

She takes a bite. "Holy fucking dog-shit assholes, man."

"Was that a compliment of some sort?"

She answers by eating with a ferocity that, quite frankly, scares me.

"More, please," she says, holding out her plate.

"Do not talk with your mouth full, young lady."

She drains her glass of water. I refill it. She eats two more helpings of gnocchi.

"You may have the rest for lunch tomorrow. Speaking of which, how was school today?"

"Ugh, you have no idea. Mr. McCauley is such a fucking perv. He's always staring at my tits. He has daughters my age. It's so gross. Oh—and *what the hell* is the deal with your driver?"

"His name is John. He is my familiar."

"Why doesn't he talk? It's so creepy. But not in a creepy way, if that makes sense. He never said one word to me. He didn't take his sunglasses off, even though it was super gloomy. *And* he wouldn't let me sit up front."

She goes on to tell me about her various other teachers and the guidance counselor who "basically lives in her asshole." There is a boy named Jason who is "obsessed" with her but, like, so annoying. The other girls do not invite her to sit with them at lunch. She eats Doritos from the vending machine by herself each day.

Afterward she goes to the sitting room and reads *Emma* by lamplight.

I hear the phone ringing underground.

✦ ✦ ✦

Jacob sounds, if not upbeat, at least better.

"So I took your advice," he says. "There was this old dude sitting on a bench at the park. And he had birdseed, like a real-life old man trope. It was wild. You never think those people really exist, you know?

"But so I asked if I could sit next to him, and there were even like other open benches but they were next to trash cans and stuff and I didn't like them. He had a newspaper on his lap and was in one of those plaid hats you see on cabbies in movies. We sat quiet for a while. I'd brought this book—it's so stupid. It's about a wizard who fights crime in Chicago, but they're actually super smart in this weird way that bends mythologies and whatever. Not the point.

"So I'm sitting with the guy, and he shakes his head and sighs, right? And so I look up. He asks me about politics and it turns out we have similar views or whatever. I thought old people were all ultra-conservative and arrogant and inflexible. I mean, my parents are, anyway.

"We talked about the environment for a long time. The question basically boiled down to this: do we have a responsibility to future generations? I said yes. Like, we deserve the same opportunities for growth that our fathers had or whatever, but look how they fucked us. We shouldn't do that to our kids. We'll probably do that to our kids.

"He said he basically agreed, but that if I was his age, I'd also understand that previous generations were mostly doing their best to better the future. They didn't fully know what they were getting into, you know? He said that parents want to secure the future, but they don't always know how. Then we talked about governments. I feel like the whole thing was pretty scattered and off-kilter, but politics are complicated, I guess. I wound up feeling pretty naive. But he was really reassuring. He said that when he was my age, he was way worse and not to worry.

"Then he thanked me for talking to an old man. That was kind of sad. His wife died from ALS, so he's mostly alone. I never had grandparents, because they all died before I was born, but if talking to him is what having grandparents is like, then grandparents are sick."

I ask, "So it was a rewarding experience?"

He tells me that it was and that they're going to meet at the same time next week to chat.

"Give me more homework," he says.

"Hm. So you have started to look forward to something. That is excellent. Do you have social plans other than this for the coming week?"

"Well, my friend wanted me to go to this Rubblebucket concert, but I don't really know them. He says they're really fun and that I don't need to know the songs, but my mind's not made up yet."

"Go. That is your homework. Lose yourself in the music. Dance. That sort of thing."

"Okay, cool."

He is silent but there is an energy of words unsaid.

Finally he says, "And, um, thanks. I guess."

He hangs up before I can say that he is welcome.

Another eight calls come in. It is a hard night for many. There is an elderly man without living relatives. He is in hospice care. His nurse will not give him the morphine overdose he desires because she is concerned about medical ethics. A middle-aged man is going through a difficult divorce. A lawyer has been laid off and claims to have no other marketable skills. A middle-aged woman is going through a difficult divorce. An alcoholic man has a stolen cell phone and a restraining order from his family. One caller in particular, however, strikes me.

Her name is Vanessa. She is a single mother who has stopped taking her medications because they make her feel not herself. She has twins. Fraternal. A daughter and a son. She is a breast cancer survivor. She works two jobs because her deadbeat ex-husband will not pay alimony.

"I'm manic right now," she says. "Not clinically. No delusions of grandeur. Just frantic. I'm fraying at the edges and the bad thing is getting closer to my core. That bad thing that Casey Anthony had. I thought for a long time about taking the kids—strapping them up—they're only two—and jumping off the roof. Then I thought about drowning them in the tub. Don't think for even a second that I don't love my kids. I do. I just don't know what to do with them. I've heard the horror stories about orphan care. My sister is schizoaffective, so she can't take them." Her voice hits a hysterical pitch. "I just can't take it."

"Vanessa. May I tell you a story?"

✦ ✦ ✦

Jeanine has asked to meet my parents.

I have met hers several times. They do not approve of our relationship. They call me things like *hebe* and *yid* when they think I cannot hear them. Or maybe they do know I can hear them. That seems more likely, on second thought.

"My mother died giving birth to me," I tell Jeanine. "My father is also dead."

"You're an awful liar."

We have met at the corner café, as is our custom on Sunday afternoons. It is brisk, but we sit outside anyway. Jeanine's beauty never ceases to amaze me, even when most of her is concealed beneath a thick coat, scarf, and wool hat. She is always beautiful to me.

"Jeanine—" I am the only one allowed to call her by this name; to everyone else, she is Jennie "—have I told you how wonderful you look today?"

"Flattery won't get you out of this." She smiles and flips her hair. "And I know." She smiles wider, knowing that now I will tell her anything she asks. "Why don't you want me to meet him?"

"He is not a good man."

"Neither are my parents. Do you think what they say about you doesn't bother me?"

"Well, I have not accepted your Lord and Savior Jesus Christ into my heart. Who could blame them?"

She laughs. "You're awful. Really and truly awful. Tell me why."

"He was not good to me. We do not speak."

"But you know where he is?"

"Yes."

She places her hand over mine. "You can't avoid the past. It just makes the future harder. Knowing where you come from, for me, will only strengthen our relationship. For better or worse, I'll love you more for it."

"And you say *I* am awful," I mutter.

"You are. So if your father is worse, you'll look better by contrast."

"If you say so."

My father lives in a squat, rented house on the outskirts of the city. We take a taxi there. It is expensive. Jeanine pays. We stand on the curb looking at the house.

I tell her I do not want to do this.

I say he is probably drunk anyway.

"He will not even recognize me. If he remembers he has a son at all."

She says, "Only one way to find out."

"He only even lives here because he sued the state. He kept saying he would use the rest of the money to start a company."

"Come on."

"That was three years ago."

Jeanine takes my hand and leads me up the walk. There is a warmth in her grip that makes me want to forgive her for bringing me here.

We approach the door. A man with the beginnings of a hunchback opens it. He squints at the light; his face is gaunt. There is vodka on his breath. He is still broad in the shoulders but seems shorter than he once was, though memory can play tricks on one's perceptions. He demands to know what we want.

My father has never asked questions, only made demands.

Jeanine introduces herself as Jennie.

I make harsh eye contact. "Father."

"Son."

Jeanine looks between us.

"You're exactly what I heard you were," she says, slipping lightly over the threshold in the narrow space between my father and the doorframe.

He does not acknowledge her passage.

He tells me it's been a long time.

I tell him it has.

"Go away," he says. "And take the trollop with you."

"She's a respectable woman."

"Enters a man's home without an invitation."

We hear Jeanine busying herself inside.

"Come in, then," my father says, slumping away.

He sits in a battered recliner. His home is desolate. Pipe smoke hangs in the air. A baseball game plays on the radio, distorted with static. I am not interested in the game, nor sports in general. This has always been a disappointment to my father.

Jeanine crashes about in the kitchen. I wince. My father kicks out the footrest of his recliner and takes a tumbler of clear liquid from a side table. I sit on a squashed, lemon-yellow couch and cross my ankle over the opposite knee. I am familiar with this couch from sleeping on it for many years. It is still uncomfortable. There are vodka bottles in the corners of the room. Dim lamplight just touches the empty containers. A revolver lies in plain view on the coffee table.

Jeanine enters through the small door that separates the living room from the dirty kitchen. She carries a tray with steaming mugs of tea.

"You have food in here," she says to my father. "May I cook you something?"

My father mumbles for her to do whatever she'd like, then

returns his attention to the game.

After some time, he says to me, "Tell me why you're really here."

"Jeanine wished to meet you."

He snorts. "So you're dating a goy whore."

"Father, I will ask you, once, to mind your tongue."

He rises from his chair, neat vodka rolling in its tumbler. "You won't do anything about it."

I sip my tea thoughtfully. "I am not a child anymore."

"But you'll always be a coward."

I stare up at him. "If you say so."

I drink more tea. He sits back down.

"Have a drink," he grumbles.

"I have one, thank you. You should try your tea. It is excellent."

He pours vodka into the tea and sips.

"It *is* excellent." His voice is a cruel jeer.

I sit in silence, listening to him curse the ballgame. After what seems like a very long time Jeanine emerges with two plates in hand and one balanced on her forearm. Whatever it is smells wonderful.

"I whipped this together from the very strange assortment of ingredients you had. Someone needs to teach you how to shop for groceries." She looks hard at my father. "When is the last time you've eaten?"

He shrugs. She places the plate on his side table. I retrieve two snack tables from beside my father's sofa and Jeanine puts our plates down.

It is gnocchi gorgonzola.

"Eat," she tells my father.

He pulls the plate onto his lap, takes a tentative bite.

He says it's good. Tells Jeanine she's lucky he thinks keeping kosher is for saps and continues eating. Jeanine conceals her pleasure well. No one speaks. My father finishes his meal and clatters the plate onto the table. He ignores the napkin. Jeanine starts to stand. I place a hand on her thigh and kiss her gently on the cheek. "Please," I say. "Allow me."

My father's face becomes a dark mask.

"A woman's work for my son," my father mutters. I ignore him and leave with the plates. "Can't teach the whore her place," he says. He raises his voice as he turns on Jeanine. "Goy trash."

I hear a sharp crack and turn. Jeanine has slapped my father. He stands and looms over her. I put the plates down and return to the couch.

"A big man now, eh?" Jeanine says.

My father's face turns bright red. He raises a gnarled hand to strike her. I sit down and sip my tea. My father swings at Jeanine's head. She steps swiftly away. My father, from his years of drinking, does not have much left in the way of balance. He stumbles forward. Jeanine sticks her foot out. My father trips and lands on his hands and knees. He spits on the floor and levers himself back to his feet.

Jeanine picks up my father's revolver and spins it around her finger by the guard. She checks the cylinder and unloads the weapon. The bullets drop into her palm.

My father looks at Jeanine in consternation and disgust.

She shrugs. "My dad used to take me hunting with him a lot."

"He has a bitch fight his battles," my father says to no one in particular.

"I would not call her that if I were you," I say.

Jeanine tilts her head at my father. "Sir, I'm currently holding your gun. Do you really want to keep calling me names?" Her attention turns to me. "Maybe I should reload this thing. Can I shoot him?"

"It seems that would defeat the purpose of our visit, no?"

"I don't think so. I've met your sweet daddy. That was the point."

I sip more tea. "Do you think we will have a warm and loving relationship with him?"

She says we can revisit that conversation if he behaves himself.

I stand and wipe my mouth. "It was good to see you, Father."

Jeanine asks if my father can be trusted with his gun.

I say we should not risk it. She hands me the revolver. I salute my father with it and take Jeanine's hand. I conceal the weapon in my waistband. We depart side by side.

We walk at a brisk pace down the street. We stop. Jeanine holds my face.

"You were right. He is truly an awful man."

I nod.

"But you." She kisses me long and hard on the mouth. "You are wonderful."

✦ ✦ ✦

Vanessa listens intently through the story. "Your father sucked."

"He was a hideous person. He did what was within his means to break me."

"This woman seems to think you turned out all right."

"There are times when I believe she may not have been entirely wrong."

"So what are you telling me?"

"Your children have long lives ahead of them. They may turn out just fine, no matter how chaotic things seem right now. It is possible that my father did the best he could, that he was simply too damaged to be better; I will never be sure. But he did not kill me, and therefore I had a chance at finding happiness and success in time. It is a parent's job to provide at least that much."

"You're an old man?"

"Yes."

"Did you love him?"

"The war was hard on his generation. He was not the only one affected."

"Your mother?"

"I never had the pleasure of making her acquaintance."

"So he was a single father."

"Yes."

She exhales. "What happened to him? If you don't mind telling me."

"Would you actually like to know?"

"Yes."

"He drank himself to death, left me as a grown orphan. Not a day goes by that I do not miss him."

This is a lie in its entirety. I do not wish to speak further of my father's death.

"Okay. Okay. Can I call you again if I need to?"

"Of course. That is why I am here."

She thanks me through tears and promises she will try to get some sleep before returning to her job at the diner in the morning. I ask if her children will be looked after. She tells me her brother is taking them tomorrow; since he bartends at night, he is their daytime caregiver.

✦ ✦ ✦

"Sounds like your dad was a real dick," Margot says.

"Keep reading about Mr. Woodhouse."

"He's super annoying."

"Yes."

"He's a nice guy, though. More or less. Hey, I wish you had a bathroom down here. I hate running up and down the ladder every time I have to take a piss."

She departs to relieve herself.

Rich calls. I quietly explain Margot's situation.

"Do you think that was a good idea?" he asks.

"It is too soon to tell. At the moment, I believe so, yes."

"Giving back is good. What you did to Jerry is bad. There were other ways."

"Not that I saw."

"You don't really believe that."

"You are the one who would know."

"Be better."

"I am trying."

✦ ✦ ✦

Margot finishes *Emma*.

I tell her she is a fast reader.

She says English is her best subject. That and math. Then she says she is tired but wants to see the coffin that I sleep in before she goes to bed.

She allows my silence to answer, leaves. I listen until I hear Margot snoring from her bedroom. Then I get a bright light and make sure the last of Jerry's blood really has been cleaned from my floor. I do not want Margot to think of this house as a place of violence.

If she does not already know the truth.

✦ ✦ ✦

The following night I wake to find Margot perusing my bookshelf. She is dressed in a T-shirt with a cartoon of Kurt Cobain smoking a cigarette, jeans she has veritably shredded at the knees, and Converse sneakers, all over which she has written profanity in silver marker.

"This stuff is all old," she says. "Why don't you read anything, like, modern?"

I tell her it is comforting to know that some things will never change.

"Is that why you're trying so hard not to?"

"I do not think I like that perception of myself."

She shrugs. "I liked *Emma*."

She removes a cigarette from her pack. I pluck it from her hand and break it in two. She removes another and we repeat the exercise.

"I thought you would enjoy the novel," I say.

"What else you got? I want a recommendation."

"Do you have a preference in subject matter?"

She chews her lip. "Do you have anything . . . happy? I liked . . . I like the ending to that last one. Where everything sort of works out or whatever."

I nod and run my thumb across the cracked and broken spines. "Something by Voltaire, perhaps?"

"The *Candide* guy?"

"So you know of him. That is a small solace, at least."

"We were supposed to read that book last year or something."

"Did you?"

"Nah. I hated that teacher. Mrs. Brown. Huge bitch."

*Candide* falls into my hand, then Margot's.

"Try it. I believe you will find it rewarding. If stylistically not very 'modern.'"

"So it's boring."

"No. It is insightful, if at times idealistic in a way you may not find, based on your opinions of Anne Frank, realistic."

"I don't want to read this. Give me something else."

"That is my recommendation. Feel free to try something different if you would like."

I turn to proceed upstairs.

"Make a deal with me and I'll read this."

I turn back. "My assumption is that you have something in mind?"

"You need to read *Harry Potter*."

"Harry who?"

"Potter. Ya kidding? You don't know who Harry Potter is?"

"Young lady, in case you have not noticed, I live underground, trying to convince people not to kill themselves. It has been a long time since I have read anything at all."

"But there are, like, eight movies, too."

"It has been even longer since I've seen a film."

"Okay, okay. That's just ridiculous. Give me like ninety bucks and I'll go get you the whole series."

"Hm. And you think I have ninety dollars just lying around?"

"You can't have time to go around hypnotizing *everyone* you owe money to. How do you keep the electricity on?"

"Fine. I consent to your terms. Dinner?"

"Oh, hell yeah. And you're *paying* for the books. I like the clothes, don't get me wrong, but even I know that stealing is, like, wrong. Ethically speaking."

There is a large jar full of cash in a cabinet to the left of the fridge. I remove it and tell Margot not to steal from it, that it is there in case of emergency. I transfer some of the money to a wallet and we set out walking. The night air is warm, according to Margot.

The children who are drinking on my hill scatter, some fully clothed, others in their undergarments. Margot covers her mouth and laughs into her hand. Marijuana and cigarette smoke mask the odors of fresh flowers and grass.

Some of the children simply watch us pass, lying unbothered on their blankets.

Margot nudges me in the ribs. "You're just going to let them use our lawn like this?"

"They are hurting no one but themselves."

"Right, I get that, but like, how are you going to spew the shit you do to callers and then let these kids, like, do drugs and shit right here? Aren't they, like, killing themselves by inches or whatever?"

"Inches are better than miles."

"But I'm not allowed to smoke my cigs or weed when you're around? Come on, dude."

"You are my charge. These other children are not."

We walk the forty minutes to the closest bookstore. Margot assures me they will be open until eleven. I tell her I *must* be home by eleven.

She sighs. "So much for our night out. But it's only eight. You'll be fine."

We enter a two-story building. The store has electronic reading devices displayed on a white table just inside the front doors.

"Maybe we'll get you a Nook instead of paper books. I can just download things for us that way."

"My home has a nook. It is in the living room. Did you not notice it?"

"Oh, my God. That was the worst joke ever. You see the signs. Don't be such a prick."

"If you learn not to be so rude, I will consider it."

"Anyway, no one really reads *books* anymore. It's all electronic. Convenience rules America."

"How very insightful."

"Yeah, I'm real fucking smart. My looks are only half of it. I read this article about how, like, romance novels have never sold better. 'Cause no one knows what you're reading on these things. So you don't have to be embarrassed reading about, like, throbbing members in public or whatever. It's cool, I guess. Get to live your life how you want without worrying what everybody's thinking all the time."

I pick up one of the e-readers. A detailed picture of the man Margot affectionately calls "Billy Shakes" comes up as a detailed illustration. She unceremoniously dismisses a store worker and walks me through how to use the device.

I scowl. "Interesting. It is like a handheld computer."

"Yeah," Margot says. "But it doesn't have, like, the romanticism of a paper book, you know?"

"I suppose. However, the purpose of books is to convey ideas through narrative, and—"

"Christ. And I thought I just sounded pretentious. How about we just go get the regular books, okay?"

She leads me to the back of the store, to a section decorated in colors that look inspired by Dr. Seuss. Bright, primary colors which assault even the senses of the dead. There are novelty mirrors, too. Margot notices them.

She tells me I can wait away from the mirrors, then disappears and comes back quickly with a stack of seven hardbacks.

"Children's novels?"

"The first one is for eleven-year-olds, the second for twelve-year-olds, then so on and so forth, up to seventeen or eighteen, I guess. That way, when they came out, kids could feel like they were growing up with a friend. Also, they made you feel like maybe you were special, too, and taught you that life is hard anyway, even if you *are* special." She clears her throat and looks away. "Real smart marketing, releasing one every year or so. Good plots. Pretty emotional. Like magical kids' mysteries. I mean, the bad guy—snake-faced dude named Voldemort, total Nazi prick—is really one-dimensional, but they're kids' books, so it works. The twists are really good, too."

She dumps the books into my arms.

"The last books are substantially thicker than the first."

"Can't expect eleven-year-olds to read 800-plus pages."

"The paperbacks would be cheaper."

"These'll look better on your shelf."

"Yes. All right."

We walk through a bargain section with puzzles, toys, and hardback books. The books apparently didn't sell in a timely enough fashion to command prices higher than their paperback counterparts. Margot examines some figurines with large heads and eyes on small bodies, makes a disgusted sound.

"We just *have* to give kids garish shit."

We proceed past the escalators to the front desk. There is not one person waiting to check out. There is, however, a full café on the other side of the store. The tables are full of people with coffee, working on their laptop computers. The main purpose of this place is clearly not the sale of books. Margot walks around the rope without following it.

The cashier tries to convince us to sign up for a membership. I politely decline and pay for the books, then receive them in a large plastic bag with a paper stabilizer in the bottom.

Margot tells me about her day while we walk home. Then she tells me I am a good listener, simply because I have not interrupted her story. "The guys I know," she says, "they always have to give their two cents and, like, relate. Which just means saying something about themselves to make you think they have a bunch in common with you or whatever. You're just quiet, or you, like, ask appropriate questions, I guess."

I nod and allow her to continue her tirade about how Mrs. Wright (the guidance counselor) took her aside today to ask if Margot was doing okay. Mrs. Wright said it was nice to see Margot smile. Mrs. Wright told her she had a beautiful smile. That seeing it was brighter than not.

Margot says she isn't sure if Mrs. Wright is just trying to fuck her at this point. Since she's "so up in my asshole all the time."

Mrs. Wright makes Margot sit in her office for an hour a day so they can talk. Margot spends that time with her arms crossed, not speaking, while Mrs. Wright switches between asking prodding questions and working on her computer.

My charge takes a cigarette from her pack. I pluck it from her fingers.

She tells me how annoying that is.

"Those things will kill you."

"I'm old enough to know that you should, like, take small pleasures wherever you can get them."

I pluck the next from her fingers as well.

She curses me and stows the pack.

I ask her why she does not petition to become an emancipated minor.

"Like a legal adult or whatever?"

"Yes."

"Because lawyers are fucking expensive, dude."

"There are lawyers that work pro bono."

"Ew."

I sigh. "Pro *bono*. As in, for free."

She scoffs. "I know that, obviously. I was making a joke. It was funny because boners are funny. Lighten up."

"Is your mind perpetually in the gutter?"

"Hormones, man. What can ya do?"

"Hmm."

The children who scattered earlier have returned to my hill. They pay us no mind this time, either higher or drunker or hornier than before. It does not truly bother me. Margot makes a comment about self-medicating, realizes her hypocrisy. She backpedals by turning the comment into a joke about getting a new weed hookup from one of the smokers.

I do not laugh.

She catcalls and whistles at the interlopers. Once she darts from the path to menace a couple on a blanket at the edge of the woods. They jolt to attention and stop their coitus. The girl hides her chest and the boy his genitals. They hastily cover themselves with their blanket.

Margot asks them not to stop on her account, reaches down to shake hands.

They do not oblige her.

"Good technique," she says. She looks at the boy. "More torque in the hips, though. Don't be afraid to, like, get in that clit either."

"Hey," the boy says, "what the fuck? Get out of here."

The girl stares at Margot with murder in her eyes.

"Now, are you kiddos using protection, or—"

I reach Margot just in time to prevent violence. I take her by the arm and she allows me to lead her away.

She complains that she was just starting to have fun.

# Chapter Four

Blood steams in a warm mug. Leftovers never taste as good as fresh food, but they are still sustenance.

I tell Margot to put *Candide* down. She is sitting in the parlor, chewing her fingernails and attempting to spoil her dinner with snack cakes. She scowls at me, says, "Shut up, I'm reading," and looks back to the text.

"Stand up, young lady. It is time for you to learn a skill. I will not continue to cook for you if you are not willing to learn how to do it for yourself."

"Teach a man to fish? You're the worst."

She slams the book down, stands next to me.

I tell her we are making boliche tonight.

"And just what in the fuck is boliche?"

"It is a pot roast stuffed with ham, seasoned and cooked with whatever you like. We will be using a rub and roasting the meat with mushrooms, onions, and carrots."

Margot swears and demands that we get to it already.

Under my careful directions, Margot cuts a smoked ham steak into long strips while I core the roast. We then run the strips through and rub the meat in a garlic and oregano paste. It is designed to enhance and complement the meat's natural flavors. We set the meat in a roasting pan and put it in the oven, set to 275 degrees.

"Three and a half hours from now, dinner will be served."

Margot stares up at me. "Three—and a half—hours? I'm fucking hungry, dude!"

"We have ingredients for salad."

"Salad? *Salad*? I have, like, I don't know, five years left of this blessed metabolism or whatever. And you want me to waste it on *salad*? Fuck off."

"Are you quite done?"

"Yeah."

"In other countries they eat dinner rather late. I will leave you to it."

She sighs and opens the fridge, removing romaine lettuce, tomatoes, shredded cheese, onions, and cucumbers. She gets croutons from the cabinet.

I make a balsamic vinaigrette in assistance.

She thanks me and places a tentative hand on my shoulder. It makes us both noticeably uncomfortable. I inform her that I will be at the phone if she needs anything.

"Why don't you sit up here and read with me for a bit?"

There is an imminent sadness to the request.

"Bring your lantern downstairs. Resist the computer. Unfortunately, you are not the only one who needs me."

Margot sighs.

I ask her what is the matter.

"I don't know. You're, like, kind of wonderful, or whatever, I guess."

I say that she is also wonderful, in a way she may not yet understand.

✦ ✦ ✦

Jacob is my first call. He is yelling at me before I can finish my opening spiel.

"Listen to this fucking day I had. Just fucking listen to it. Jesus Christ. What a fucking day I've had."

Nothing is said for a bit.

"Are you there?" he demands.

"Yes. I was under the impression you were going to continue shouting about the day you have had."

"Right, yeah. So I worked from home. It was a reward from my boss for calming a client down so we didn't lose them. But so I've been selling some of my old shit on eBay, trying out a more minimalist approach to life. I know that sounds pretentious, but I'm over caring about how I sound."

He is not over it.

"So I had to go to the post office to ship out some of this shit. And I've been there, I don't know, like a hundred or more times. Probably a hundred fifty, I don't know—"

"Jacob."

"What?"

"Are you high?"

"Oh, dude. I am so high. I needed to get through the night, you know? I got this weed pen with oils in it. Science is fucking crazy. I'm super hungry now, but I have a pound of this really good chocolate from an old-school candy store. And I ordered a tuna hoagie from this place that makes the most amazing fucking hoagies. But so what?"

"Nothing. Continue your story."

"All right. Where was I? Oh, right, so I'm on my way to the post office. And I've been there like at least a couple hundred times, maybe like three hundred, I don't even know. I decide to walk a new way because with all those trips I'm tired of seeing the same shit.

"Now, in my neighborhood, even though the city's a grid, the streets bend and whatnot. They get kinda hard to navigate if you take the bendy ones. So I take one of the bendy ones and I get to the street with the post office. But because of that bendy street I turn the wrong way on Franklin, the post office is on Franklin, I don't know if I said that.

"Now I'm walking, right? And I've got these big headphones I like to wear. So maybe I shouldn't because they make me unobservant or whatever, and I don't pay enough attention. I could get mugged or something, but I like my music and it makes the walk go by faster. Anyway, it was the middle of the day."

I offer murmurs of acknowledgment throughout.

Jacob says, "I hit Franklin and make the turn but the wrong way. But I have my stupid fucking headphones on, and I'm like, 'Okay, this doesn't look super familiar but whatever, I'm walking a new way.'

"And I walk for like fifteen minutes before I'm like, 'This is totally wrong.' So I finally plug the address into my phone. That's when I realize I've gone the wrong way—which is annoying, but not a huge deal. I overdressed for the weather with a jacket and a hat and my big headphones. I'm sweaty from this backpack full of old shit that I'm selling. A couple old hockey jerseys, some collector editions of video games, that sort of shit.

"I'm sweaty and annoyed and I get to the post office half an hour later than I want. This means it's now right during lunch. Everyone else who fucking needs the post office is there on their lunch break. I wait behind like ten people. Not a big deal either, right? The clerks, though? Slow as shit. Slow*er* than shit.

"And so then I'm waiting and waiting. I'm checking email on my phone. I haven't missed anything from work but I'm getting antsy. Now, after forty-five minutes at the post office and seventy dollars in shipping charges—but those charges don't matter since I charge for them on eBay—anyway, now I'm tired and more than just a little bit annoyed.

"I go to get coffee at this place across the street from the post office. I like it there. It's one of those hipster places that lets dogs inside and everything. And there are usually cute girls and the food is pretty decent. The coffee, though, is real, real strong, which is what I like. My roommate's working from home, too, so I offer to grab an extra coffee. He needs hella cream and sugar. I drink mine black. But so I have to fill his to the brim with half-and-half and pocket four Splendas.

"I wanna smoke a cigarette while I'm walking, so I figure I'll hold my coffee and put his in this mesh cup holder in the side of my backpack. Everything is ready to go and predictably I drop his coffee all over the floor. Now I'm mortified and all and this dog comes up to lick the coffee and cream from the floor. I don't know a super lot about dogs, but it can't be that good for them.

"Then this weirdly hot Asian barista comes over—I say weirdly hot because Asians aren't usually my type, but she's got this desperately gorgeous Filipina complexion and long lashes and her body is kickin'. So I'm into it. Oh, plus her hair is dark up top but pink at the ends, adding to the weird aspect of the hotness. She comes over with a towel to wipe up the coffee. I offer to help, which she seems vaguely appreciative of.

"Now I'm just apologizing over and over and over, which obviously annoys her, but she gives me a new coffee for free, probably just so she can send me on my way. This time I carry both cups because of the spill and not wanting to further embarrass myself in front of Weirdly Hot Asian. This means I can't smoke my cigarette.

"And because my roommate needs more fucking cream than coffee in his coffee, I keep spilling onto my hands because the cup is so full. My roommate thanks me or whatever and asks why I've been gone so long. I'm pissed from this whole ordeal and toss him the Splenda and slam my door. I don't even wind up doing any work because now I don't feel like it.

"Then I fall asleep and wake up and I feel guilty because I was a dick to my roommate. Then I order delivery—not DiGiorno—and get super high. But now I feel shitty all around so I called you to bitch about it, because I know nothing that happened was a big deal, but it legit has me wanting to end everything just so I never have to get so annoyed again."

I tell him that there is no need to cry over spilled coffee.

He says *ha*, *ha* in an emotionless sort of way. He eats something that makes a loud crunch with each bite.

I begin to ask a question.

He cuts me off.

"Yes, you can tell me a goddamn story."

✦ ✦ ✦

This story about Rachael predates the altercation in the park. She has been showing for a few months now. We sit at her table with our tea.

"He's kicking."

This is before ultrasounds could predict a child's sex. Rachael refers to the child as "he" as a prayer. Why she would pray for a boy is beyond me. I do not pursue the line of questioning.

She says, "Here, feel," and places my hand over her bulging stomach.

I feel nothing.

She laughs. "He never kicks you."

I smile and lean back in the chair, sipping my tea. "Why don't you move?" I ask.

"Because no one has come around and dropped the money for a new home in my lap."

"Come live with me."

"In that awful apartment with the moldy furniture?"

"We can bring your furniture, if you like."

"Then there seems to be little point in moving at all."

"All these steps are not good for you."

She tells me I live only one floor lower.

I say nothing.

We sit in silence for a long time before she asks me to leave. I walk down the eleven flights of stairs. My knees perpetually ache these days from my rigid back and its uneven pressures. I hit the street and am greeted by a rain heavy enough to soak through my clothing. A Ford automobile splashes me on the sidewalk.

It is not a wonderful day.

I arrive at my apartment. My neighbors, an elderly couple with identical stooped postures, greet me.

The husband, Gilroy, asks, "Why the long face?"

His wife, Marilyn, tells him not to pry.

They bicker.

I ask them how they are doing.

Gilroy says, "Old."

I tell him he sounds like a spring chicken.

He rolls his eyes.

Gilroy and Marilyn make me smile.

They come in for dinner. Stiffly moving through the room decorated with the aforementioned moldy furniture, Marilyn complains about her husband's irritable bowels and asks that the food please not be overly seasoned. Gilroy demands some red meat. Marilyn snaps at him.

I make chicken with mild seasoning and sear it on both sides. Marilyn bustles home and returns with spinach salad so that she can teach me her recipe for balsamic vinaigrette. We sit and eat. I say little. They say many things. They ask how far along Rachael is, tell me to enjoy it before "that little bastard pops out and you never sleep again."

Gilroy and Marilyn talk for a long time about how I should marry Rachael, just to make things official. They tell me that they know we're decent people and that they don't give a damn what anyone else thinks. They say that getting married would make things easier, though, when it comes to the rest of the world.

Gilroy says, "As far as I'm concerned, their right to wave their fists stops at your nose."

Marilyn sighs. "Remember how everyone talked after we had *our* sweet little bastard, dear."

Gilroy grunts.

I tell them I will think about it.

They thank me for my time, say it is getting late. (It is 6:45 p.m.) They go home.

The springs in my couch are mostly broken. It makes sitting very uncomfortable. Nevertheless, I sit there for a long time.

It has not been an ideal day, but there have been much worse. Marilyn and Gilroy have brightened it considerably.

✦ ✦ ✦

I ask Jacob to tell me one good thing that happened to him today.

"This tuna hoagie is crazy fucking good."

"And have you had days without crazy fucking good tuna hoagies?"

"Yeah."

"That is the point. There is something enjoyable in your day. Focus on that, as opposed to the bad. As my foul day was improved by a quiet dinner with kind friends."

He pauses. "Okay."

"Do you feel better?"

"Moderately. What happened to Gilroy and Marilyn?"

"Marilyn fell down the stairs several weeks later and died."

"Gilroy?"

"Starved himself to death without her."

He sighs.

"Jacob, have you tried anything new in a while?"

"No. Just lying in my fucking rut."

"Well, then. I had a thought about you."

He says just how fucking sweet that is.

"Go to a yoga class in the morning before work."

"Uh, no thanks."

I say he could use some spiritual alignment. Plus, it may be a good way to meet new people. He agrees, then holds the phone to his rear end and farts into the speaker before hanging up.

✦ ✦ ✦

"They're gonna move me," Rich mumbles.

"To where?"

"Dunno. Somewhere new."

"Are you allowed visitation tonight?"

"No."

"I'll be over in fifteen minutes."

"Thanks."

Margot puts down *Candide*. "Field trip?"

"Not for you."

"Can I answer the phone?"

An unexpected request.

"No."

She shrugs, says whatever, tells me she should get some sleep anyway. I disconnect the telephone, follow her up the ladder, and see her to bed. She mutters "good night" through half-closed lips.

There are signs of someone trying to break into the heavily padlocked room at the end of the hall. Margot will have to be reminded that this is unacceptable behavior. A key hangs on a chain around my neck, sitting in the rotting hollow of my chest. I fit it to the lock; the padlock snaps open and falls into my palm.

Inside the room, dusty frames holding black-and-white photos rest on once-polished furniture. I pick one up. A girl, curly-haired, with a smile that crinkles bright. But her eyes, gazing into the distance, are sad. A much younger version of me stands beside her, with a hand on her shoulder. A child, in the human sense, stands between us, a tiny tuxedo straining across his broad shoulders.

I set the photo down and open the closet.

It is filled with finery from long ago, but there is also a modern, navy-blue suit hanging above a pair of dark-brown wing tip shoes. The jacket's lapels are narrow, the pants tapered at the ankles. A white shirt with thin blue stripes hangs within the jacket. The outfit is a bit loose on me but will look full to the human eye. I tie a full Windsor in a brown tie patterned with small blue diamonds.

Not having the option to check my appearance in a mirror, I depart.

The behavioral center where Rich lives is a stout, brown building. The front doors are locked. A sharp knock on the glass rouses a desk guard, who rubs sleep from the corners of his eyes. He motions for me to leave but meets my eye in the process. His jaw slackens. He opens the door, asks if I would like to come in.

I do not need a formal invitation to enter this building, but manners matter.

I thank him and tell him where I wish to go; he leads me down a long hallway. The building's interior is done entirely in neutral colors. We pass a small courtyard, outside to our left, with paths that converge in the center and a cement walk running the perimeter. It has trees and green grass, so during daylight hours it seems like a pleasant place. It is quite different by the light of the moon, however.

The guard passes a plastic card over a sensor and a mechanical lock slides open. He pushes the white steel door open for me. We pass a darkened room with rows of padded chairs, several circular tables, and a television hung high on the far wall. Light shines to our immediate left: the nurses' station.

There are three female nurses, all slender, all tall, all young, seated at intervals behind the desk, checking paperwork and yawning. A stocky boy in a tight black T-shirt, tattoos on his arms, approaches.

"No visitors at night, John. Who is this?"

The guard, his jaw still hanging loose, says nothing.

"Who are you?" the boy asks me.

He makes eye contact and his jaw slackens too.

The nurses look up, tired and confused. Their eyes meet mine one by one. I tell the tattooed boy to lead me to Rich.

Rich is strapped to his twin bed. He has no roommate. His grey eyes are bloodshot. He is emaciated and his hair is plainly unwashed. He wears pocketless blue scrubs with no string at the waist, socks with rubber on the soles, and a white T-shirt with holes at the collar.

I enter the room with hands folded behind my back.

"Show me," Rich says.

I drop my glamour.

"You look terrible."

"Are there mirrors in here, or are they afraid you'd smash them and use the shards to slash wrists and throats?"

"Polished steel."

"So then you are able to see what you look like."

He grunts. "They don't let me shower. Keep getting turned around, doing it with my clothes on."

His restraints are very tight. Bruises encircle his wrists. The buckles are thick but come undone with stiff pulls. Rich sits up, rubs at the marks.

I ask him what happened.

He tells me that one of the other patients took his chess pieces. When asked about it, the other patient told Rich he ate them with his mac and cheese. Unconvinced, Rich asked him again. This time, the other patient told Rich he shoved them up his ass. Rich was unamused.

"Guy does card tricks all day," he mumbles. "Annoying. Steals things. Moment of weakness." Rich shakes his head. "Moment of weakness."

The straps at his ankles wrap around the bed to the same effect as the wrist restraints.

"To where are they moving you?"

"Long-term care. One call a month."

"And this and the chess pieces spurred your altercations?"

He nods. "At least they let me call before buckling me. Nice of them. Nice people here."

I tell him to stand up. His stench wafts with his movement.

I tell him to shower.

I tell him I am not interested in seeing him naked but that I am not comfortable leaving him alone.

Rich is tall, towering over me in a way that suggests an ancestry of warriors or athletes, if that distinction can be made.

He is thin, malnourished, but wiry. I walk into his bathroom. Water drips in fat beads from the shower faucet. The water runs hot after several minutes.

I ask him to please wash himself.

He nods, mumbles thanks, says he has no soap.

I walk to the front desk where one of the young nurses produces a small bar of soap and travel-sized bottles of shampoo and conditioner.

A loud bang issues from Rich's room.

The polished steel above the sink is dented. He tries to slam his head into it once more. His neck is thick but graspable. A sharp squeeze catches his attention. He looks at the blank space where my reflection should be in the distorted disk.

"Did a bad thing."

His forehead is already swelling and dotting with discolorations.

I say firmly that it is time for him to shower.

He strips and enters the curtained stall. I sit on the toilet beside the shower and cross my legs. He moves to close the curtain, but I catch it.

"Water gets everywhere," he says.

"I do not trust you."

"Lie."

I sigh. "I do not trust you not to harm yourself given the smallest of opportunities."

He acquiesces and stands under the steaming water.

He says, "Take our strings. Our shoelaces. But leave curtains. Could hang myself just as easy with one. If I wanted."

"Do you want to?"

He nods.

"My offer stands, you know."

"Not safe."

"I am aware."

He smears soap over himself in a scattered fashion, squeezes the entire bottles of shampoo and conditioner into his knotted hair, lets the water wash the chemicals into his eyes. I frown but do not intervene. He stands in the hot water for a long time. He tries to turn the temperature as high as it will go. It is already hot enough. I readjust it for him.

Rich turns the water off and stands dripping and naked, stooped and defeated.

"Would you like a towel?"

"They have those too. Long enough to tie. Easy to kill yourself."

"You have had a rough few days."

He nods.

"I am here for you."

"Why don't you lie when you say that?"

"Because it is true."

He looks at me long and hard. "Last time you killed someone?"

"The girl's foster father."

I move at top speed to procure his towel and return. He takes a step over the shower's lip onto the soaked floor. He dries himself quickly. His clothes, lying on the bathroom floor, are soaked through, but there is another pair of scrub pants waiting for him in a cubby hole beside his bed, along with a blue V-neck T-shirt made of reinforced paper. He shrugs the shirt over a back distorted by burn scars and deep gashes.

Rich sits heavily on his bed. He makes eye contact with me. It does not affect him.

"I don't want to leave here," he says.

"That can be arranged."

"Too many people involved. You wouldn't be able to. Things

would go wrong. Have to leave anyway. Not worth it." He doubles over, chest between knees, feet spread wide apart. "Does anything good ever happen?"

"Yes."

"Lie."

"You know it wasn't."

"Made me feel better."

He looks up from between his knees, a manic grin spreading over his features.

He asks if he can tell me a story.

"I do believe I have heard it before."

Rich adopts a slightly British accent. "I do believe it would be of the utmost usefulness for me to impart this particular story upon your ears, again, so that you may be reminded of the goods and evils of the world in which we reside. I wish to anecdotally tell you of how our actions require penitence for true atonement if we are to ever forgive ourselves."

"From where the fuck did that come?"

He shrugs. "Story?"

✦ ✦ ✦

Rich is an unstable boy. Labeled at an early age. Never gets the chance to break out. Bad grades in school. Speech impediment. Put in special classes for nonverbal kids. He's verbal, but it comes in waves.

He's frustrated. He's angry. He's condescended to. He knows it but can't express himself. His family's dysfunctional. A counselor says maybe his condition is genetic. Rich doesn't know what it means. It's not explained to him. His adults say he wouldn't understand the concept anyway.

At home, Rich is fostered by a kind old woman. Rich loves her. She lets him watch the black-and-white TV channels with her. They eat microwaved dinners on trays.

School is not like home. Rich is often restrained at school. He kicks shins (a tendency that I for some reason find hilarious). One day, one of Rich's teachers decides he's tired of bruised shins. He decides to teach Rich a lesson through pain. The teacher assaults him in a sterile white classroom. It's their one-on-one time. The teacher tells Rich he's no good and stupid. Rich kicks him. The teacher doesn't like that. He punches Rich in the face, grips the teenager's throat.

Rich is already a large child. Taller than his teacher and well-fed. Rich has what some faculty refer to as "retard strength." He gets angry. He grabs the teacher's throat back, with two hands. He knees the teacher in the balls. The teacher falls. Rich doesn't let go of his throat.

Rich sits back at his desk and waits. He cries. Another teacher notices time is up. She enters the room. She sees the body.

She screams.

Rich panics. Rich sees red. Rich is having his first full-blown psychotic episode.

He just wants the teacher to stop screaming. He starts babbling. He swings a chair.

Rich is already a large teenager. Well-fed.

The second teacher falls. Guards walk in. They have blue jackets and electric cattle prods. (There have been incidents at the school before. Administration does not see the electrified poles as an excessive means of restraint.) Rich grabs the prod from the faster guard. He headbutts him in the bridge of the nose. He rams the prod through the other guard's eye. The first guard is lying on the ground. Rich kicks him repeatedly in the head.

Rich staggers from the room. He is confused, covered in blood.

✦ ✦ ✦

Rich finishes the story. His cheeks are wet with tears.

"What can I do to make you feel better?"

"Tell me about Rachael."

✦ ✦ ✦

Rachael is still the most beautiful woman I have ever seen. She has only grown more attractive with age. Her mid-forties have been kind. Her eyes are bright in contrast to the worry lining her forehead, the crow's feet.

We sit on furniture bought with my father's money. The boy in charge of finance for my father's company—a business for which my father shows an uncanny acumen—has put away substantial reserves. This way my father cannot drink all the money away. I am paid a salary much larger than my nominal position merits. It is either an immensely kind gesture from my father or an attempt to emasculate me. I do not care which.

The money allows me to provide a home for Rachael. And our son.

Our house is two stories, dark blue with a slate roof. We live in semi-isolation: there are no neighbors within a quarter of a mile. Rachael grew up wishing for a lawn to watch from a high window. Our back lawn stretches a hundred feet before shifting into dense woods in which we collect firewood. Only a narrow dirt road leads up to the secluded property.

Rachael sits outside on the porch each morning with her tea. Our son sits beside her. He is a quiet boy with blue eyes, the promise of broad shoulders, and feet that are large and wide.

He reads and sips tea also. I love him. Rachael speaks philosophy to him. He nods and listens. He reads *A Connecticut Yankee in King Arthur's Court*. He likes the stories of Camelot and satire in general. Rachael rises to greet me, kisses me tenderly on the cheek. We go inside to listen to the radio. She dances and sways in the wooden living room. Our son walks in, smiles. The three of us dance.

I pirouette in an ungraceful impression of a ballerina, ignoring the physical pain it causes. We collapse on a Victorian sofa, laughing. Rachael wraps us both in one-armed hugs. I stare into her eyes, their ever-present sadness mixed with a relief that will last at least another hour.

She is not always a happy woman. But by the grace of the Lord, she makes it work.

✦ ✦ ✦

Rich sits on his bed, still crying. "Lie."

"It was not."

"Just that last part."

"Perhaps. Will I hear from you?"

"Have to come visit."

"I will." I tell him to call me at the first opportunity.

He promises. "Don't kill anyone on the way home."

I don't even want to.

Lie.

After retrieving the address for Rich's transfer destination, I leave.

✦ ✦ ✦

The hill upon which the Tudor mansion stands is deserted but for one group of children stinking of whiskey. They have drugged themselves to sleep.

I am hungry. Rich's words rattle around my brain. Sunrise is imminent. The kitchen is clean but for an overfull trash bin. I quickly heat a pan of blood and drink it down. It is not a satisfying meal.

✦ ✦ ✦

Margot has been waiting in the sitting room to complain that *Candide* was a total letdown.

"It was super boring and philosophical. And then, like, what? They wind up farming? Fucking *farming*? How is that optimism? Candide's life sucked."

"Candide was a man of conviction and responsibility to his ideals."

"Pangloss was an idiot, El Dorado is a myth, and Martin was the only dude in the book who could actually think. It's anti-Semitic *and* I could keep trashing it if I wanted. I mean, Candide gets his skin whipped off just because he's in the wrong place at the wrong time? And then he murders people, but Voltaire is all like, 'He's the most noble of creatures, blah, blah, blah.' Terrible book choice by you. Just fucking terrible."

She wears a hooded sweatshirt with sleeves that allow her thumbs to poke through at the ends. In her hand is *Stranger in a Strange Land*.

She says she feels, like, connected to the title.

I inform her that it is a dated and sociopolitically problematic novel.

She says that she's in the mood for some science fiction and my library is woefully insufficient where this genre is concerned.

The wrapper of a hoagie and an empty bag of kettle-cooked potato chips lie crumpled on the island.

She belches and informs me that she made her increasingly creepy driver stop at the grocery store on the way home.

"Maybe your next read should be *My Fair Lady*."

In a Bostonian accent, she says, "Maybe go fuck yaself."

"That is incredibly rude."

"Dude! *The Departed*. You've never seen *The Departed*? Have you been living under a fucking rock?"

"A hill, actually."

"Yeah, fair enough. Did you start *Harry Potter*?"

"I have not."

"I read *your* shitty book."

"It is not shitty."

"Whatever. I'm gonna go take a shit and then you're gonna watch a movie I downloaded."

I frown. "I thought I was supposed to be reading about a child wizard."

She shrugs. "You'll be up all night. Do it later."

She goes upstairs. I go downstairs. She meets me in the sub-basement, wearing her down jacket and what appears to be several pairs of flannel pajama pants. Her hood is tightened around her ears. The computer's mouse rolls at her touch and the monitor flashes to life.

I ask how she proposes to comfortably watch a film in this bare room without a television.

She looks around. "A TV would be better, but we can put the monitor on a chair. And maybe bring some furniture down here. Also, why are you still using a landline? And wearing that douchebaggy hat. And that telemarketer headset. You look crazy."

I blink.

"Can you put that glamour thing back up? I'm sick of looking at you. And get a space heater."

"Any more demands?"

"I've been living here for like a week now. It's time to step up your technology game."

I say that sometimes it is nice to be reminded that old things still work. Especially at my age.

"Okay, well, at my age, I like cool shit. You have none."

"Learn new ways of amusing yourself."

"Fine. But there's a lot of space down here. Can you bring down one of the couches from upstairs?"

"Yes."

"Do you need help?"

I scoff at the word *help*.

The Victorian sofa does not fit through door frames. I kick them out as I proceed through the house. It is cathartic, in a way. Margot has dragged the computer desk out of the corner, pulling its power cord taut. The couch crashes down before the new setup.

"A new computer wouldn't kill you, either," Margot says. "This one's slower than snails covered in syrup."

"What a pleasant image."

"Come on, you have to be getting used to it by now. I'm charming, in a kind of gruesome, raped-a-bunch-of-times type way."

"That is not even moderately humorous."

She falters. "Whatever."

"Turn on your film."

She clicks through a menu.

The film is called *The Royal Tenenbaums*. It is told in chapters opened by a library book. The style of cinematography is interesting. It often focuses the characters' gazes directly into the camera, giving the audience an uncomfortably close look into their eyes. The story is about a family and the mental illnesses brought about by eccentric parents and the children's own natural abilities.

It is a sad film, but redemptive and subtly hopeful.

Margot gives her opinions throughout. Wishes for popcorn, or at least some Twizzlers, or whatever. But she's still full from dinner so she can make it through, she guesses.

She elbows me in the ribs while an actor named Luke Wilson stares at his own reflection.

"Pay attention," she says.

He says, "I'm going to kill myself tomorrow," into the mirror.

He sets about cutting his hair and beard with scissors. A song by a musician named Elliot Smith, who died, like, way before his time, plays. It is a terribly sad song.

Luke Wilson finishes grooming himself, takes a razor. The screen flashes entirely red. The film cuts to him lying on his bathroom floor with blood streaming down his arms.

I tell Margot that I do not think I am a huge fan of this film. I say I do not appreciate how it seems to romanticize sadness. I ask if this is appropriate viewing for someone her age.

"Just wait. It's beautiful."

By the end, I agree.

Margot does not watch the ending with me. She is asleep with her head on my shoulder and a tiny string of drool hanging from the corner of her mouth. I carry her to bed, check the locked door at the end of the hallway, and return to the subbasement. Seven books about a child wizard lie beside my phone. It rings. I answer.

A boy says, "This is an emergency hotline, right?"

"Yes. Please let me know how I can assist you."

He clears his throat. "Well, I took this pill. And it says to call emergency if the . . . uh . . . erection lasts for more than four hours. I think I might be in some trouble, here."

"Sir! Call 9-1-1! This is not the appropriate line."

"Right. Right, right. Sorry. Bye."

It does, in a rare fashion, feel like a potentially happy, peaceful night.

# Chapter Five

I finish the first *Harry Potter* novel. I find it to be dissatisfactory. It is hard at my age to relate to books written for eleven-year-olds. However, I do appreciate the hope the young wizard seems to inspire in his friends, and I applaud his change in circumstance.

I begin the second book.

The phone rings. I am thankful for the distraction.

It is a boy called Jamar.

He is a college-educated poet. He is not entirely convinced that I can be of any help.

"I cannot pretend to understand your circumstances, but I will try."

"You gay?"

"I am asexual."

"Interesting. But no one's going to hate you out of hand for that."

"This is true."

"You know what happens to gay Black boys in America?"

"I cannot imagine that it is good."

"Yeah. It's not. Every single day I have to be reminded that I'm Black. That I'm gay. That I fit into very few communities. Man, even the music I listen to's coated in homophobia because of all this toxic masculinity. You know how many fights I got into in school? You know how many extra kicks they'd give me in the chest on the playground? You know how many times I've been pulled over because my windows don't have as much tint as me?"

"Not unless you tell me."

He goes on to talk about how abnormal he is made to feel in America by the news, by his peers, by the sublimation of hundreds of years of systemic racism.

He says, "Academia treats me like my voice doesn't matter. All they teach us is the writings from these crusty old white dudes and make excuses for their racist-ass shit by saying they're a product of their time, like that excuses this shit. The literary canon is full of the same five writers over and over again, man. And they cling to these old-school rules of grammar that don't matter for true communication, you know? I don't understand why, if my writing's clear as fuck, they have to knock points off my grades because I used a comma instead of a semicolon. I mean, what the fuck is that?"

He says he's tired of it all.

I tell him exhaustion is a part of life.

He talks for a long time about how giving up would be nice, but that it isn't an option, not really. He tells me a story about a white girl who tried to "turn him." She told him he was racist for not sleeping with her.

He says, "Like me being gay had nothing to do with it. She called me a big black buck. Asked why I wouldn't just wanna get it no matter what. Like she wasn't trying just so she could tell her future husband about how she slummed it way back when."

I hear him shaking his head.

He asks if he can read me a poem he wrote earlier tonight.

He opens with a caveat that it's a first draft, but says I'll get the point.

His voice shakes as he likens Black boys to Atlas, the permeating message being that human beings aren't Titans. That he is not a Titan. That he doesn't know how long his spine can take the weight.

"I'm gonna slam that poem," he says.

I tell him he should.

I ask if people really snap when they like things.

He laughs. "Yeah, they do."

I ask if anything in particular happened today that has him feeling suicidal.

He tells me to point to a day on a calendar. Something happened that day to make him feel suicidal. His father died last week.

He says, "It's been hard."

"Death always is. Would killing yourself cause your family more or less pain?"

"More. But it would end mine. I feel like that's selfish. Then that feeling compounds on itself and makes it worse. Then it makes me more depressed. Where's the out?"

"I do not often tell callers this, but I killed myself once."

"Pardon?"

"I killed myself."

"You mean you tried to kill yourself."

"I mean I succeeded."

"Oh, cool. I'm talking to a ghost then." He says to himself, "This bitch thinks he's a ghost."

"No. You are talking to a vampire."

"Sure. So now you're gonna try to convince me I'm crazy and that all the sad is in my head. Man, you're vain as fuck."

"I am telling you the truth."

"It wouldn't make sense even if there *were* such a thing as vampires."

"How so?"

"Vampires gotta be turned by vampires. If you killed yourself, you wouldn't have had the chance to be turned."

"There is a grace period."

"Man, stop fuckin' around and get on with it."

I say, "My point is this. I spend every day wishing I could go back and not kill myself. Unfortunately, death is not a temporary condition."

"Do you think I'm stupid?"

"I think you are tired."

"That's because I told you I am. It was like two minutes ago. I was there when it happened."

I ask if I may tell him a story.

✦ ✦ ✦

Jeanine needs to talk to me. About what, I do not know. It sounds urgent. We meet at our corner café. Her dog, Solomon, is tied to her chair and sitting politely.

I go to kiss her. She shifts her cheek into the path of my lips.

"Is it finally happening, then?"

Her eyes well up. "Just sit down."

I do. She does not meet my eyes.

"You need to understand that I love you. More than anyone I've ever known."

"Yes."

"Don't do that. Don't be crass."

I ask her if she will look at me. She does. I smile. It is not a convincing gesture.

"When did you decide?" I ask.

"Last night."

"We could be happy, you know."

"You could. And only you. You don't know how important family is. You can't."

No one knows how important family is better than someone without one.

I tell her she is probably right.

"It's just the whole Jewish thing. Oh, god." She covers her face with her hand. Solomon whines and drops his head on the ground. "My parents would never forgive me if we—if we got married."

She places my grandmother's ring on the table.

I place my hand on hers, tell her I understand.

Something beautiful breaks.

"I want you to know," she says, "that this is my choice. Not Daddy's or Mama's. Mine."

The beautiful thing goes up in flame.

I cannot form words. Hot tears run on my cheeks. I take the ring and put it in my pocket. It has the weight of a dead star.

She tells me that his name is Charles Calder. That he works for her father's practice. That her father thinks the world of him. That he can take the Eucharist without sacrilege.

She says, "I'll always love you."

But he is more appropriate.

I stand up, my nose running. Jeanine watches, her eye makeup dripping.

I kiss Solomon on his blocky head and croak, "Goodbye."

I am not invited to Jeanine and Charles's wedding.

✦ ✦ ✦

"Experience is merely the name men gave to their mistakes," I tell Jamar.

He is quiet for a long time.

"That's not the quote," he says.

"What?"

"*Dorian Gray*. That's not the quote."

I laugh despite my desire not to. "No?"

His voice is deadpan. "The real quote is, 'Experience was of no ethical value. It was merely the name men gave to their mistakes.' Right?"

"Yes."

"And they say an English degree's not worth shit."

"My version was snappier."

"Whatever, man. I've got an issue with that sentiment."

"Go on."

"So if experience is just mistakes, and the presumed nature of a mistake is that it's bad, then isn't the ethical thing correcting that behavior?"

"I would have no choice but to agree with that."

"So there *is* an ethical value to experience, and that dude is just making excuses for shitty behavior."

"Hence my shortened rendition."

He snorts. "Nah, but here's what I'm saying: if it were true that experience has no ethical value, if it's just a euphemism for mistakes—which are like, *mistakes*, errors of judgment, not things you do that are shitty and wrong—then everything is subjective."

"You do not agree that it is?"

"No. No way. If all morality's subjective a murderer can say there's nothing wrong with murder because *he* sees it that way. So for his code of ethics, he hasn't done anything wrong. There wouldn't be any good or bad. Everything would just be what it is without any standards. Nothing matters."

"What about cultural differences?"

"Well, that's why there's war. Hate. All that. One nation says things are this way, another says they're that, and they both think they get to decide. And of course they say what's 'right' is what's in their own interests. Objective morality would say to serve the best interest of your fellow man, regardless of geography. Pure egalitarianism. But that's not happening anytime soon. Hey, you're Jewish, right? You support Israel against Palestine?"

"I support resolution of conflict. Bombs are bombs, aggression is aggression, and people are people. The violence is the problem, regardless of the reason for it."

"I can get on board with that."

"Would you like to talk about your father?"

"Nah."

"Okay."

He says, "He was the best. Really. Filled the room with love and jokes and made you feel safe no matter who you were. You were Black, he loved you. You were white, he loved you. Asian, Spanish, one leg, three tits, whatever, he loved you. He might fight your ass, but if you weren't hurting other people, he loved you."

"It sounds like you loved him very much."

"*Love* him. I love him very much. Not many fathers I know are supportive of their gay poet sons. But he knew what being marginalized was. He'd talk shit. This, that, and the third. But man, he was exceptional. He made sure that no matter how they treated me, his light was always there to lead and support me. Now that light's dimmed, but it's never going out."

"That is a nice way to look at it."

"I don't know what your deal is with this vampire shit or anything, but thanks. I feel better. A little, anyway. Let me ask you something."

"Of course."

"You ever eat anybody?"

"Yes."

"Dark meat?"

"Not usually, no."

"Why not?"

"In my early days, before I found alternatives to unnecessary killing, I used to hunt Klan members."

He whistles through his teeth. "For real?"

"Yes. May I tell you why?"

"Because they're racist dickheads?"

"There was another reason as well."

"What's that?"

"It was fun."

✦ ✦ ✦

Margot is curled up on the couch in front of the computer. She is wrapped in several blankets and has placed the monitor on the floor so she can look down upon it.

"Hey," she yawns.

"Good evening."

"I didn't like that Heinlein book."

"Did you finish it?"

"Yeah. All that bullshit about no one can die." She makes a farting noise.

I tell her Heinlein was likely not a wonderful man.

She says yeah, he was totally a she-was-asking-for-it misogynist and a homophobe and a racist.

She says, "I liked one thing about it, though. The quote about love. The one where 'love is that condition in which the happiness of another person is essential to your own,' or whatever."

"Thou art God."

"Yeah, I didn't get that part. It just sounded kind of lame, like a cliché."

"I see it differently."

"How's that?"

"Think of the idea of God. God is an omnipotent creator who acts on the universe and shapes it according to His or Her or Their or Its will. Humans are the creatures with the most agency on earth, or at least that is what empirical evidence suggests. Agreed?"

She rolls her eyes, nods.

"Then, with respect to Earth at least, humans are the most godlike of beings."

"Whatever."

"Eloquent. What are you watching?"

"Nothing worth explaining." She leans down and presses the monitor's power button. The screen blinks off. "I need to, um, talk to you."

"We talk every night."

"No, idiot, I need to *talk* to you *about* something."

I tell her I am confused.

She asks what else is new.

She rubs at her wrists.

She stares at the floor.

"So, um, my English teacher, Mrs. Deangelo, she like, uh—" she clears her throat "—wants to talk to a parent."

"I see."

"During the day."

"What is this about? Can John not usurp the position?"

"John? *John*? Señor Fucked-Up-Face, Never-Talks John? No. No, I don't think he'd be great for that."

"About what would she like to speak to a parent?"

"My schoolwork."

"Are you failing?"

She coughs into her hand. "Not exactly? I guess you could say, that, um, since you, like, ***kidnapped*** me, which you totally did, by the way, I'm sort of—excelling. Her word. Not mine."

"Then what is the problem?"

"Well, she seems to think something's up, right, and it's super unfair, but she thinks Jerry is gone—maybe 'cause of some stuff I said, I don't know—anyway she says that if a parent or guardian can't come meet her, she'll have no choice but to get someone involved. Like, a new social worker or something."

"I've been wondering about that, actually," I say. "Don't you have an assigned social worker who makes routine checks?"

She scratches at the back of her neck. "Yeah, once upon a time, in a galaxy far, far away. But social workers don't get paid so much, you know? And Jerry *really* didn't wanna lose his stipend for taking me in. So they made an arrangement. This piece-of-shit, I-don't-want-to-do-my-job-right-and-maybe-call-the-cops asshole worked it out with Jerry that he'd sign saying everything's okay for a cut of the money. I assume he's too scared of Jerry to check in and see why the money's stopped."

"That seems quite awful."

"Well, yeah, it is, but I can't totally blame the guy. Jerry told him he could have either a cut of the money or, and I quote, 'your asshole torn up through your throat.' Charming, I know. But given the options, it's, like, understandable, I guess."

I tell her it is still not acceptable.

She asks me if there's like any kind of solution that pops into my head.

"Otherwise someone's gonna go visit an empty apartment and things could get really awkward for me. And then for you, I guess."

"Are you . . . threatening me?"

She waves her hands in front of her. "No. No, no. It's not like that. Really. I'm just saying that those are, like, the circumstances of the predicament." Margot chews her thumbnail and looks down. "I'm really sorry. Like, really. But I don't know what to do." She begins to cry. "You've been, like, so good to me, and I don't want to, like, put you in a terrible position, I just don't know what else to do if you can't make it."

"Margot—"

"Margie," she corrects me, eyes momentarily narrowed.

"Margie, relax. I will meet with your teacher."

She looks up, her eyes magnified by tears. "Seriously?" She then hugs me. "But how?"

"Tell your teacher that I work during the day but would be happy to meet her at the school in the evening or have her for dinner."

She rolls her eyes. "Have her for dinner?"

"That is an old and bad joke among the undead."

"You wanna hear a bad joke? What did Cinderella say when she got to the ball?"

"What?"

Margot chokes.

"How vulgar."

The tears are a thing of the past. Margot laughs aloud. "But seriously," she says when she catches her breath, "don't invite her over here for dinner. Then she'd know where I'm staying, and I don't need that noise. Maybe we could clean up Jerry's apartment instead? Nah, never mind—cleaning it would be a total pain in the ass. Let's definitely try the meeting at the school thing. I just don't know how late she'd be able to stay, is all."

"Can we not just set up a phone call?"

Margot shakes her head, scratches her neck, and paces. "Can we throw a tarp over you or something? To go out in the sun?"

"We are better than that."

"Yeah, true."

She offers several more ideas for bringing me safely through the sunlight: carrying a super-big umbrella; spackling my body; wrapping me in toilet paper like a cheap-ass Halloween mummy costume.

I find none of these suggestions to be particularly satisfying options for safe travel.

She claps her hands. "I know! We'll blot out the fucking sun!"

I tell her my patience is running somewhat thin.

"Yeah, no, I get it. I was just thinking, ya know, vampire. Maybe you guys have supervillain-type weapons or something."

"We do not."

"All right. I'll see if I can set something up, tell Deangelo that you have to pay the bills and everything and can't leave work. That she can't come here or anything because you're scared of strangers."

"Scared of strangers?"

"Whatever. I'll think of something better. It'll be fine."

The last sentence is said out loud to self.

✦ ✦ ✦

Jacob calls, says he's been focusing on the positive. He sucked at yoga but there were "girls with butts" there. His therapist thinks this is a wonderful idea. She's happy that he has started taking her advice to heart. He tells me that the girl he likes, the same one that he is in love with but in denial about it, texted him yesterday.

"It wasn't even anything important. She just texted me, 'Hey.' But it was at 3:00 a.m. Hashtag she's thinking about me."

"Hashtag?"

"Don't worry about it. Anyway, I keep having these awful thoughts about ways to kill myself and making up plans, but they're passive ideas now. I'm always having those thoughts. They're sort of ever-present. I bought a gun last week, but I don't wanna use it or anything. So that's good."

"Did you meet the friend you made in the park yet?"

"*Yes*. Dude is the fucking man. Did you know he was in Auschwitz? Like, *the* Auschwitz. He even showed me the tattoo of his numbers, which was terrifying, but he laughed it off and told me about how he *escaped*. Bro, my man escaped Auschwitz. Grabbed a rifle, killed some Nazis. Like some straight-out-of-Tarantino shit. I mean it had to be a tall tale, right? Or just straight-up lying to hide the awful truth, or whatever. But it was still a great story."

"Sounds very interesting."

"It was. And not only that, my dude has a granddaughter, and she's a smoke show."

"Smoke show?"

"It means she's hot. She comes to get sweet old grandpa, because he's legally blind and can't drive—which he says just comes with getting old, but his dick still works, so things could be worse. He's *hilarious*. Anyway, he's got this smoking hot granddaughter. And who's there looking all sensitive and cool with her grandpa? Ya boy, Jake. That's who."

"Well what about this other girl you like?"

"What about her? I'm biding my time. That doesn't mean there aren't other girls out there. This granddaughter, Lucy, totally seemed into me. My confidence is off the charts right now."

"That's excellent to hear."

"Yeah. But so, like, the whole time, all these suicidal ideas are still bothering me. Not a huge issue, but they're still there."

"Take your mind off it. Do you want to hear a story?"

"Honestly? Not at all."

There is an awkward silence as I search for words.

His voice turns excited. "I know what there is. Let me tell you about this wild fucking dream I had."

"Of course."

"Okay. Settle in. It's a doozy. And it's super weird. Total mindfuck.

"So it starts out where I'm still in college and I'm coming home for some unknown reason. And I get to my parents' place, only it's not the same. They've come into, like, billions of dollars, with a *b*, but they never told me. I'm thrown off and a little pissed.

"They're living in this monster complex of a house with granite and marble and high-tech shit everywhere. It's an interesting aesthetic, to say the least. I look out the window and there's this giant military base that they built next door—I shit you not, the wall, in big yellow letters, just says *Army* on it.

"Anyway, I head up this gigantic spiral staircase to my room. My room, despite the overhaul of the rest of the place, looks exactly like my room from before. Only it's giant, with a two-hundred-inch flatscreen in the corner, which is touching, I think. And in my room are all these fucking nerds I grew up with. Most of them are younger kids from my neighborhood. They've got sixteen people in there playing GameCube, which is an old gaming system that only takes four players, but they're all playing just the same.

"So I'm like, 'The fuck you guys doing in my room?' But they're all excited to see me, which pisses me off more. Not sure why. Then I'm screaming at them to get the fuck out of my room. They all scurry off, terrified. In my dreams, I'm an intimidating man. Now they're all gone and I'm in my room alone. There's an exposed toilet in the corner of the room, just chilling there.

"Suddenly I have to poop. I strip naked and sit down to take a shit. The door, which I forgot to lock, flies open, and there's the girl that lived catty-corner to us. Weird, because we never really talked. I cover up my junk and politely ask her to leave. But she's like, 'I just have to change,' even though she's as embarrassed as I am. She gets naked in front of me and then puts her same clothes back on and leaves.

"Now I'm magically dressed without having done it and my parents are throwing this monstrous party. Every single person I hate from high school is there. There are these three massive dance floors in their billionaire complex. These dance floors have real stereotypical club feels, with the alternating blue, red, and purple lights, and there are DJs and bars packed with liquor.

"The important part about this is I hate clubs. And I'm furious because my parents invited all the people I hate. I don't go say anything because they must be having fun somewhere and I don't wanna ruin that. But I can't go to bed because the music and shouting is so ungodly fucking loud.

"I head to the top-level dance floor and there's this forty-year-old guy that I swear I've never seen before in my life. He looks like a pretty accurately aged version of myself. Except he's got the ultimate-douche chinstrap for facial hair and a stud earring and an Atlanta Braves hat with the sticker still on it. But then he's also got a baby stroller that he's pushing through the dance floor like it's no big deal. The stroller's empty.

"He gets right up in my face but doesn't say anything. So I'm like 'whatever' and head farther into the club. Gracefully, my parents did manage to invite a couple people I like. We all sit on this blue suede couch in the middle of the room. We watch everyone dance their foreplay dances, right? Then I'm with my buddy Hank and a bunch of girls we went to college with. I went to this school that was like 70 percent girls and most of them are hot, so we're all dancing. This girl I had a crush on grabs me around the waist and we're doing the whole R. Kelly 'I don't see nothing wrong with a little bump and grind.'

"And this girl, whoa boy, what an ass on her. In real life, too. We're going at it dancing and I'm finally starting to have fun at this ridiculous party. Then, lo and behold, fucking old-douche-lookalike-me is there with his stroller. He's staring bullet holes in my head. Then this girl I'm dancing with spins away and jumps into his arms. They're making out and basically fucking with their clothes on. I sit back on the couch and my friends keep dancing. I'm drinking heavily and everything is fine, if a little dull.

"Now here is where things really start to go off the rails. All of a sudden these demons—they kind of look like Chinese dragons with ghost tails, but some of the faces are more fucked up and classic Pan-goat-demon types—they start coming out of the walls. They start straight-up slaughtering people. Real gruesome, where even though it's a dream, I'm like, 'Fuck, that's messed up.'

"The even weirder part? Everyone at the party is totally cool with it. Like this is the highlight of the party. Meanwhile, people are having their heads chopped off and being eaten and there's blood and dirt and shit everywhere. But I'm bored. Probably something in there about being too desensitized to violence, but who am I to say?

"So I walk down this other giant staircase because I'm done watching the demon murder show, and the whole house has blood and dirt and shit all over the white floors. I walk through the kitchen, where a bunch of the demons are eating people. The demons nod at me, which makes me feel super fucked up. At least they don't want to demon-rapture eat me or whatever it is they're up to.

"The kitchen—and this won't mean anything to you, but it's just a huge version of my cousin Scott's kitchen—fades away and I'm in an equally fucked-up study with floor-to-ceiling bookcases. My dad is sitting on his ruined couch, reading the newspaper, even though no one reads newspapers anymore.

"He folds it on his lap and asks if I'm having fun. And instead of being like, 'What the fuck is this?' I just shrug and say sure. I tell him I'm going to bed. I walk past the dude with the stroller. My college crush is gone. The dude watches me go to bed. We don't see him for the rest of the dream, but I feel like he was important to this first act. Whatever.

"I go to sleep, in the dream, like I'm in a Christopher Nolan movie where everything is super confusing. But so I go to sleep and wake up. My room is back to its normal state that I grew up in and I think to myself, 'Oh, okay, that was a super-weird dream.' I walk out of my room and none of it was a dream. There's still blood and dirt and shit everywhere. Except the kitchen. The kitchen's pristine and there's a line of a couple hundred people waiting to get to this buffet counter.

"I come downstairs and they see me and all cheer 'Pastries!' like they've been practicing. I cut the line because fuck them, I live there. There's one guy in the way who's trying to decide what to eat. People are polite enough not to go around him but not nice enough to abstain from ridiculing the shit out of him. I grab a plate and go on my merry way. And that's the whole party scene."

I ask him how he remembers all this.

He tells me he keeps a dream journal because the only time he gets to be truly creative is when he's asleep.

He says, "That's not everything, though. You have time to hear the rest?"

"For this, I have all the time in the world."

"You're psychoanalyzing me right now, right?"

"It is extremely hard not to."

He laughs. "So now I'm in school, and it's my first-grade classroom, but I'm the age I am now, not in college anymore, and I have untreated PTSD or something from the demon murder party. I'm hallucinating in class and throwing punches at demon images. But really I'm just punching the shit out of my classmates. Obviously, they're all getting pissed. No one fights back. They don't want to fight the crazy PTSD kid because it feels wrong to them or something. Then I'm holding this bichon frise by its neck and I'm shouting, 'Does anyone else see this dog?' And everyone else is like, 'Nah, dude, ya crazy.'

"Now cut to me in a hospital for people with drug problems and hallucinations. Everything is weirdly beautiful, like a rehab center in a Showtime show. I'm sitting in a circle at a group therapy session. Next to me is like the hottest girl in the entire world. It turns out she's a porn star, but she's totally my best friend in the hospital. We lean on each other emotionally while we're there. We never fuck, though, because that's the reason she's in there or something.

"This is fine with me because she's a genuinely great person. That's that. There's this special rule at night, just for me, where they let me into this colosseum-like courtyard. There are steps all around it and giant glass windows up above. All the other patients and doctors and nurses watch me every night, to monitor my progress or something, probably. The reason I need to be outside is so I can take my pants and underwear off, but I leave my socks and green T-shirt on and run around the courtyard with my hands in the air, screaming, 'I'm free,' over and over.

"Then I wake up. I have no idea what happens after that. I don't know if I ever get out of the hospital. I don't know how my parents got their money or where the demons came from. There's no real ending. No revelations."

I ask him if he is taking any anti-anxiety medications.

"A shit ton."

✦ ✦ ✦

Vanessa calls. Her children are asleep but she has long since stopped resting.

She asks me if I have children.

I tell her I had a son once upon a time.

"What happened to him?"

✦ ✦ ✦

Michael is eleven years old.

He and I sit in amiable silence. Rachael is working late at the hospital cafeteria.

A knock comes at the door of our house. It is a large boy in a white tank top.

He is the boy of my nightmares.

He is the reason for my stiff back.

He is all smug smile and wide shoulders.

"Michael," I call. "Go to your room."

"Let me in," the rapist says.

"No, thank you."

He does not enter. This is a surprise.

"I want my son," he says.

I tell him Michael is not his son. I want to look him in the eye to tell him this, to stand my ground as a man and defend my property and family. However, I am, after all, a coward. I stare at his sternum.

He laughs in my face. "Does pretending he's yours make you feel like you can get it up now?

"Leave this place and never come back."

"I don't think so."

Michael has not gone to his room. He stands behind me. He looks at the stranger curiously.

"I'm your real father," the rapist says to him.

Michael only asks his questions with looks, though fortunately he does not like to look at the faces of strangers either.

I tell my son to go to his room.

The rapist asks him if he can come in.

I tell my son not to answer. He runs up the steps.

"I want my son," the rapist repeats.

"We all want many things. How was prison?"

"Not fun."

"How awful for you."

"I've got a bone to pick with you because of that."

Absently rubbing my back, I say, "I have several to pick with you."

"Try me."

"No, thank you."

"I'll get him whether you want it or not."

I take my father's revolver from a drawer beside the door. It is only now that I smell offal on the rapist's breath. I point the gun at him. He smiles. His canines are pointed.

✦ ✦ ✦

"And?" Vanessa asks.

"And I gave my life to save my son."

"Would you do it again?"

I think for a long time.

"I think so, yes."

"What if I gave mine to save my children from myself?"

"I would not advise such an action."

"They're in immediate danger from me."

"They are in immediate danger from many things. Please, call 9-1-1 if this is an emergency."

"I think . . . I think I'll do that."

"Please do."

She releases a cry of anguish and hangs up.

# Chapter Six

The next night I prepare to go see Mrs. Deangelo on behalf of Margot. The girl is visibly nervous. She changes outfits half a dozen times in search of something that makes her look "wholesome" before settling on the tropical dress I picked out for her and a white cardigan sweater.

I tell her to sit in the living room. I rifle through my wardrobe. I have no frame of reference for this kind of meeting. In despair I put on my finest tuxedo, come downstairs.

"Um, Daddy Warbucks," she says. "Try again."

"I do not like *Annie*."

"Yeah, me neither—I mean, I've never even seen it really—but that one song about the sun coming out, everyone knows that one. There's this comedian I heard say that tomorrow is relative. Like, on Monday, Tuesday is tomorrow, but when you get to Tuesday, Wednesday is tomorrow. That means the sun doesn't ever get to come out. Makes the whole story a lot more hopeless if you think about it that way. Although I guess that would be better for you—the sun never coming up, that is."

I shrug. "So what is the proper attire for this sort of thing?"

"Ugh."

She goes upstairs and returns with a button-down shirt, which she has managed to leave unmarred, and a pair of black jeans.

"What are these?"

"I snuck them into the shopping carts in case you ever needed to dress, like, *well*."

I frown. "I prefer how my own clothing looks. If memory serves, of course."

"Tough. Change. And let me know when you're finished."

I go into the master bathroom. I call out that am dressed.

Margot enters and tells me to sit down. There is a stool in front of the vanity. She fusses about in the cabinet and comes out with makeup. She makes me face her.

I ask, "What is this?"

She says that she wants me on my A-game. That if keeping up the glamour uses too much energy, this might be easier. That she appreciates me coming. That she thinks this will help.

She spends the next twenty minutes powdering and painting my face. Her hands, as she positions me, are soft and firm. It is uncomfortably intimate, with her examining the lines of my face closely. I do not like how gentle her touch is. It takes an effort of will not to recoil. It makes my face feel tighter than usual.

She says, "For fuck's sake, can you look at me? I need to get under your eyes."

Our eyes meet. I know those eyes too well. I pull away from Margot. She pulls me back and holds my face still. When she is done painting me, she steps back and tells me that it's great, that I look sixty years younger.

I am fairly certain she is lying, but there is no way for me to verify.

Margot clears her throat. "Nah, who am I kidding. It's not even close to good enough. You still look totally dead."

I tell her I'm sure I look wonderful.

She smirks. "Not like you have any way of knowing. But, um, yeah, probably do the whole glamour thing. We're not fooling anyone with you looking like this."

I shrug and do as I am told.

"Better," she says. "And take that stupid fucking hat off, will you?"

At this point, I am not sure I *can* remove Gordon's hat. "No. Shall we fly?"

"Um, no, moron. I told John to get us. For appearances."

"Okay."

She checks a watch. I do not know where she acquired it.

"John will be here in five. We'll meet him at the bottom of the hill. Come on."

We depart the house. Margot whistles and catcalls the children outside. One boy, a can of light beer in hand, watches her curiously. He is handsome, with blond hair swept to the side, long legs crossed before him. He holds a guitar and wears no shoes. Margot notices him looking at her.

She nudges me in the ribs and asks, "Do you see this douchey California wannabe?"

I smirk.

We reach the bottom of the hill, where John waits in a long black town car.

Margot and I sit in the back seat. John observes us in the rearview mirror, nods. His face is scarred: long pink streaks run vertically through one eyebrow and down behind his sunglasses, as well as horizontally over both cheeks. His suit is all black, no tie, black shirt buttoned to the collar.

He believes that one day I will make him a vampire.

He is very patient.

The school is a twenty-five-minute drive away, through wooded two-way streets that open onto crowded blocks and stop signs at every corner. It has a long, wide parking lot for buses. The building is Cold War era, long and low, made of red brick with a green roof. There are few windows, and even fewer of them have light shining through.

John lets us out at a sidewalk in front of the entry doors. I allow Margot to lead the way in. We pass through metal detectors that beep. A security guard does not bother to look up at the sound. The foyer has a floor of dirty tile leading to stairs with thick metal handrails. An administrative office is to our left. Margot pays it no mind.

She leads me through unadorned hallways with rows of red metal lockers. Around a sharp corner. Past a dark, locked cafeteria to a hall with a collapsible metal gate, partially closed, at its mouth. There is one room with lights on, two doors from the end of the hallway. In it sits a rail-thin blonde woman with a marker. She pores over school papers. She has thick glasses and an olive complexion. Her face is long and angular with incipient wrinkles between her eyebrows. She looks up and her eyes light in a way that suggests unexpected *joie de vivre*.

"Margie," she says. Her voice is airy. "And you must be Mr. Flurber." The teacher stands and shakes my hand vigorously. "It's a pleasure to finally meet you."

It is almost hard to find the lie beneath her exuberance.

I tell her it is good to make her acquaintance as well.

She asks us to please sit, then perches on the front of her desk. She wears an outfit very similar to the one Margot selected for me, only in brighter colors.

"I'd like to talk to you about Margie's performance," she says.

"Hey," Margot interjects. "You don't have to talk about me like I'm not here."

Mrs. Deangelo looks at Margot with the demeanor of an aunt talking to a favorite niece. She says, "Sorry. Anyway, Mr. Flurber, I've wanted to meet you for some time."

I clear my throat. "Apologies, Mrs. Deangelo—"

"Please, call me Judy."

"Apologies, Judy. I am a very busy man."

Her voice edges with ice. "I see."

"But you would like to discuss my foster daughter. Please proceed."

"Yes, well, Margie's performance of late has been excellent, but—" she turns her gaze to Margot "—there are some things I am worried about."

Margot sighs. "This again?"

"Yes. This again. Mr. Flurber—" I do not ask her to call me by first name "—Margie is very talented. In fact, she's one of the smartest students I have."

Margot mutters, "Especially in this shithole."

"Yes," Judy says. "Especially in this shithole. The nature of her work, however, is somewhat concerning." Judy brandishes a sheet of paper. "I'd like you to read this."

"You wrote this?" I ask Margot.

She does not look at me but nods.

✦ ✦ ✦

### *Tragedy Indeterminate*

*You look at tall buildings with lust. Lust is just slut with the letters screwed into new spots. Ults luts sult stul lust slut slut slut slut slut.*

*Life is only ever getting fucked into new places. Skyscrapers start to scream OPTION at you. You wonder if they're telling the truth. They nod to the beat of your heart, rhythm of your footsteps. You wonder if the fall would be exactly like jumping onto the subway tracks. When your wildest dreams at night are of killing yourself, you're bound to wake up disappointed. When you get exactly what you want, what does time matter? You'll have all the time you could ever need. Or none. But isn't that the same thing with a semantic twist?*

*You knew a boy once. He had blond hair and scars that matched yours. He wore a braided necklace from where he tried to hang himself and failed. He said that the scar tissue vaguely remembered a smile. He couldn't look in mirrors. He said the smile mocked him. Did you know they sell shotguns at Dick's Sporting Goods? Did you know the cheapest hunting option is only six hundred bucks? Plus the six-pack you buy the closest homeless guy to pretend to be your dad. If you want to make sure you get the shotgun, maybe you buy the homeless guy some new clothes. Clearance racks are full of options for men with no fashion sense. Maybe you buy the guy a can of Axe Body Spray. That sickening male hooker scent that can cover up just about anything. As long as you're okay with singed nose hairs. Altoids. All in all, Chris's death would run him, what, $638?*

*You knew a boy once. He had blond hair and a scar necklace. He had a father that made him go hunting. His father and uncle liked to go out before the ass crack of dawn to drink beers and jerk off their rifle barrels. Chris shot a buck in the head by accident. It ruined any chance of mounting it. Chris's father cracked a rifle butt over his son's head. Chris rode home in the freezing truck bed, huddled against the deer carcass, Skywalkering like on Hoth. It almost seems heroic, in hindsight. The public perception of heroism rarely means staying alive in a life you don't want.*

*Chris never wanted to kill the deer. His suicide note read:* An eye for an eye.

*You whisper, "I'm going to kill myself tomorrow," and go to sleep the day away.*

✦ ✦ ✦

I look at Margot. "Who is Chris?"

She does not turn her head to acknowledge me.

Judy says, "You can see why this is deeply worrying. Normally, I wouldn't say this in front of Margie, but she knows how I feel. Especially about those scars she's hiding."

Margot turns red and remains silent.

"She is smart," Judy says. "And special. I wanted to meet you to ask that you please keep a close eye on her. I don't want anything bad to happen to any of my students, but especially not Margie."

"Nor would I let anything harm her."

Judy purses her lips. "The one she is most in danger from is herself."

"Oh, *come on*," Margot complains.

Judy's patience runs thin. "Mr. Flurber, I simply want to make one thing clear: I am responsible for Margie while she is at school, but you are the rest of the time. Make sure she is properly cared for."

She meets my eye, gaze hard. Her jaw slackens. I sit and think.

I decide I am glad for this teacher.

Mrs. Deangelo snaps back to reality, rubs her eyes.

She tells me that she is tired and we may go. She hands Margot another copy of her paper, marked with a large red A. She tells Margot to call her if she needs anything.

We leave the way we came.

Margot tells me that she loves Mrs. Deangelo, but worries the teacher wants to be too close to her. She is not good at letting people in. She didn't know Mrs. Deangelo just wanted to threaten me. She says *sorry* over and over on the way back through the neglected metal detectors.

I tell her that it is fine, and I am just pleased there is an adult looking out for her during the day.

John's is one of four cars in the parking lot, aside from deserted school buses. John stands beside the driver's door, arms folded. I tell Margot to go to the car.

"Where are you going?" she asks.

"I could use some air."

She looks at me sideways. "You'd think that, like, with all the practice and everything, you'd be a better liar."

I repeat myself. She goes to the car. John opens the rear door and she dumps herself in. The car pulls slowly away. I turn and stare at the school doors. I walk back through them.

The guard looks up at me and then away. I go back to Mrs. Deangelo's classroom. She is packing a satchel with papers. On her desk is a stack of Norton anthologies. Mrs. Deangelo looks up at my entrance but does not falter.

"May I help you?" she asks.

I pick up an anthology and let it fall open in my hands. I see that I have turned to Joyce Carol Oates's "Where Are You Going, Where Have You Been?" I skim it while Mrs. Deangelo ostentatiously ignores me. The story is based on the incident of the Pied Piper of Tucson, a serial killer who began his career by murdering a fifteen-year-old girl.

Mrs. Deangelo finally finishes with her bag. "Do I have to ask again why you're back?" she says.

I shake my head. "I would just like to say . . . thank you. For looking out for Margot, when I am unable. Mrs. Deangelo—"

"Judy."

I sigh. "Judy, it is a great relief to know that Margot is cared for when I am not around."

Judy arches an eyebrow. "She lets you call her Margot?"

"No."

Judy snorts. "Didn't think so."

I close the book and replace it on Judy's desk.

She asks, "So you just came back in here to thank me? A phone call or an email—"

Judy meets my eye. All the liveliness slumps from her posture. She becomes vapid.

I tell her that she is to keep a close eye on Margot. That she is not to let any harm befall the girl during the hours before the sun goes down. I tell her how fond of Margot I have grown, and how upset mistreatment of the girl would make me. If any harm does come to Margot, whether at the hands of bullies, other faculty, or anyone else, I will hold Judy personally responsible. And I will return to make this school a bloodbath.

Judy comes back to herself. She rubs her temples and squeezes her eyes shut.

"Wow," she says. "Talk about a headache."

I smile. "Have a nice night, Judy. Please, don't forget what we talked about."

She shivers and asks, "What do you mean?"

I smile.

She hurries from the room, clutching her satchel.

✦ ✦ ✦

I return home to find Margot sitting outside the front door. She has a lit cigarette dangling from the corner of her mouth. She watches the barefoot blond boy play guitar and sing. She stands when she sees me.

She stubs the cigarette out on the ground.

She asks what I was doing.

I tell her there was something I forgot to discuss with her teacher.

"Whatever, weirdo. I'm hungry."

"As am I."

She hugs her arms. "I never like the way you say that."

"My apologies."

We enter the house. I glance back at the guitar player. His eyes are closed. He hums. I slam the door shut.

I go to the kitchen. I fry chicken, slice potatoes and cook them in the chicken grease, and roast asparagus with salt, pepper, and homemade balsamic.

Margot says, "No ham steak? Weird for you, man."

She plays with her food for several minutes before taking the first bite. Then her metabolism kicks in and she eats the rest of the helping on her plate. We store the leftovers in Tupperware for her lunch the next day.

There is one plastic tub of blood left in the freezer, labeled with a large AB+ on the top.

I say, "Somewhat of a delicacy, in my circles."

The blood reaches 99 degrees Fahrenheit. I pour it into a white bowl with a brown floral pattern around the rim and drink it down with two hands, feel the tight tendons of my dead body loosen. The variety of markers in the blood give it a multitude of flavors.

Margot asks me about *Harry Potter*.

I tell her if that tiny British boy can be so irritatingly optimistic after being locked in a cupboard by a cruel, deluded family for his first eleven years, I will be fine after being scolded by her teacher.

"Yeah, but he has Hogwarts to look forward to. A world of possibilities or whatever. Full of literal magic and new friends and a destiny and everything."

I place a hand on Margot's shoulder. She shivers.

I whisper, "So do you."
She chews her lips, says nothing.
I ask what is wrong.
Margot says, "Do you think I'm okay?"

✦ ✦ ✦

There is a man who works at a morgue. This morgue is on the outskirts of the city, through the Black ghettos that used to be Jewish. It is a square of white cement. There is no outdoor lighting. Morgues need very little security.

This boy, I call him Guy.

Guy is not his real name.

He welcomes me as an old friend.

He does not know my name.

His jaw hangs slack.

Our arrangement is that he drains blood and freezes it for me when circumstances allow, labeling the containers with the blood types. Once, I tried to suck the congealed blood from a corpse before he had frozen it. This was the body of a morbidly obese man dead of a predictable heart attack. The arteries were so clogged it was like trying to slurp sludge through a straw.

Margot likes to tell me that our culture loathes fatness because we think it shows laziness and lack of self-worth.

She talks about the "fatties" she knows at school, who totally hate themselves, but some of them are rich girls who know they'll buy their husbands one day. They're the ones that won't care if they're cheated on. She tells me we also hate fat people because we are afraid their influence will make us fat. I find her views to be extraordinarily closed-minded and quite vicious. She says America isn't worth shit, but she wouldn't want to live anywhere else.

I try to tell her that self-love is infinitely more valuable than a perfect body. She says whatever.

I do not think I would trade places with an angst-ridden teenager, even if it meant being alive again.

Guy brings me a stack of seven frozen tubs of blood with medical history printouts taped to their lids.

I reject two tubs.

One holds the blood of a woman killed by alcoholic liver disease. The other, that of a man who died of AIDS.

Guy caresses my face and thanks me for visiting. I pick his nose, just because. Instead of running home, I walk.

Children sit on their front stoops, playing music from speakers plugged into smartphones. Girls in tight clothes dance in the street. Younger children ride bicycles, popping the front tires high in the air.

Some drink from bottles and cans hidden within brown bags. Four large boys in their twenties stand at an intersection, shaking hands with passersby. Many of those buying drugs tremble, scratch their necks, walk in stooped shuffles. Prostitutes in fishnet stockings stand outside gas stations or lean against the walls of twenty-four-hour pharmacies shielded by bulletproof glass. It is the kind of neighborhood where people post "Beware of Dog" signs even if they have no dog.

A building has a banner that reads: *Northeast Treatment Center. Foster parents wanted.*

People watch as I walk by. A prostitute solicits me, then calls me pejorative terms for homosexuals when I do not acknowledge her. A boy stands in my way in the street. I do not break my stride. He walks away before I reach him.

The quality of the sidewalks gradually improves. There are more streetlights now. There is a football field with bleachers and a heavy chain-link fence. Buildings grow taller. A university logo rides high upon a dormitory building the size of a skyscraper. Beside the dormitory is a strip mall with a grocery store, electronics retailer, shoe store, Chinese restaurant, and hair salon. All are closed for the night.

My stroll takes me across the well-lit campus, where I pass several police officers on bicycles. There are call stations under bright lights for people in need of safety escorts. Food trucks parked on the street are closed. There is not much to do in public places at this hour. Night dwellers know this is the time to do what is only acceptable in shadow.

Dawn is approaching. The sky begins to grey. I run the rest of the way home. Having replenished the freezer, I go downstairs and see that I have missed several calls. Sitting on the side of my bed, I stare at the chains dangling from the radiator. I wonder if the dead ever really leave.

The only decoration in my room is a horse's head in profile. It is done in string art. The mane is orange and yellow, the neck blue and green, the eye white.

Artists just want to play God with lower stakes.

Thou art God.

In the words of Margot, what kind of bullshit is that?

✦ ✦ ✦

The subbasement stinks of cigarettes.

It is late Friday night, the start of the weekend.

Margot is unwashed, her face stripped of its usual paint. She has lit scented candles—from where she retrieved them I do not know—all around the room. They do not cover the cigarette smell. There are power strips attached to every outlet in the walls. The lamps from most of the living room tables now reside in my dwelling space. The computer desk has been dragged in front of the couch. On it is a large television in place of the usual monitor. Margot tells me that an HDMI cord basically lets you turn your computer into a TV because the internet will let you watch whatever you want.

I say, "It smells awful down here. Have you been to school?"

"Full disclosure," she says, "I skipped. Hold on, hold on. Before you get angry. I just needed today to decompress, you know? Deangelo was super weird to me yesterday. Like, I kept finding her lurking around hall corners and shit, watching me."

"That is rather odd."

"Yeah, she's probably just still worried, like she said. Anyway, I've been pretty fucking bored today. Porn looks crazy on a screen this big. You can really see how puckered the girls' assholes are."

"You watch porn?"

"Gotta do something when you're locked in the house not getting laid."

"You are sexually active?"

She yawns. "Yeah."

"But you are so young. And given the abuse, I would not have guessed—"

"Whatever." She tenses; her tone is hostile. "I don't need a lecture from you, okay? I did just fine for sixteen years before you came along."

"I just thought—"

"All you do is think. Relax. We're watching an action movie tonight. Oh, also—I'm sure you'll get your twat in a knot over this, Pussy McGinastein—I snuck out and got you a new phone and a wireless headset. Works off Bluetooth. You know, so you can get rid of that cheesy office phone."

"You replaced my phone?"

"Yeah. The jar didn't cover it, though. I found your real stash."

The voice in my head screams and curses her. I breathe and force control when I speak. "I told you not to go in my room."

"I didn't have anything to do today. Like, at all. And if you don't want someone getting through a lock, don't keep bolt cutters in the shed."

"I did not know there were bolt cutters."

"That would explain why they're so rusty."

"I told you not to go in that room."

"Yeah, but you tell me a lot of things." She shrugs. "Sit down, we're gonna watch this super-ridiculous Jason Statham movie. All he does is shoot people—"

"I told you not to go in that room."

"Are you mad at me?"

"Come with me."

"Wait, okay, I see that you're mad. I get it, but like—"

Something overcomes my rational mind. My vision goes red.

I shout for her to move her ass.

She stares defiantly at me.

"Up the ladder," I say. "You are no longer welcome in this house."

"You gonna fucking kill me if I don't leave?"

"I will eat you."

She spits at my feet.

"Do your worst, you fuck."

She makes rebellious eye contact. My stomach twists and writhes, but Margot's jaw slackens.

I say, "You have her eyes, you know."

She nods.

I sigh. I tell her to follow.

She mindlessly obeys.

We walk through the basement, past my bookshelf. Up the spiral staircase with the wall sconces. Through the doorframe I ruined bringing the couch down. Into the wooden hall joining the foyer to the kitchen. Left down the hallway. Another left up the main staircase. Right at the top of the stairs. Left down the hallway with the blood-red carpet to the door at its end. Margot did not bother to remove the evidence of her trespass. The broken lock lies on the ground next to the discarded bolt cutters.

The door creaks open at my touch. I notice that dust has been wiped away from the faces in many of the photographs. I tell Margot to sit in a faded armchair. I stare at her for a long time. It is a thoroughly saddening experience. She snaps out of my control. She looks around, confused, and rubs her eyes and scalp.

"Fuck you," she snarls.

"We have been through that particular line of inquiry."

"You scream at me and then bring me to the place I wasn't supposed to be? Are you gonna kill me here? Wait. How did I even get here? Did you fuck with my brain? Can you do that? What the hell, man. I thought we were, like, friends."

I hand her the picture of Rachael, Michael, and me.

She looks at it for a bit, then tosses it back to me.

"Is that Rachael or Jeanine?"

"Rachael."

"She looks like she could be my older sister."

"Yes."

"Is that why you came back for me?"

"No."

"You're a lousy liar."

"Lousy?"

"I've been trying to cut back on my swearing. You haven't fucking noticed, have you?"

"I came for you before I ever knew what you looked like, did I not?"

"Yeah. But then you came *back*. You didn't have to do that."

"You were a child, all on your own."

"Oh, fucking spare me. You call everyone children. You killed Jerry. You don't give a shit about people. You're on that dumb little phone all night. You're not rushing out of the house to help people like Batman or something. You're just a scared old corpse."

I look at the floor. "I do occasionally help people."

"Whatever. You still haven't given me any other reason why you came back for me."

I do not answer.

She asks, "This your son?"

"I raised him as such, yes."

"He looks like he could be my brother."

"Yes."

Her voice softens. "You never told me whatever, like, happened to Rachael."

"No."

"Could you?"

✦ ✦ ✦

The rapist returns to our home several times over the next few months. Michael's birthday comes and goes. The rapist never enters our home, but he never ceases to ask if he may enter. I make sure to have Michael home before sundown every night. Horror stories are scary. This does not mean they cannot be true. In fact, they should be taken for the warnings that they are.

Rachael has not encountered the rapist. Or if she has, she has not told me about it. He has a knack for arriving only when she is not there. A forceful knock shakes the doorframe. Michael goes to his room. I open the door. The rapist stands there. He is in the same tank top and the same slacks.

He asks to come in.

I tell him he may not.

He usually leaves when I threaten to send for the police. Tonight he does not.

"I'm done screwing around, pal," he says. "Look at me." He hisses, "*Look me in the eye.*"

I still cannot.

Instead I draw my father's revolver and step back from the door.

"Go," I say.

He folds his arms. "No. Why don't you come out here and talk, huh? Wouldn't want my son to hear anything bad happen to you."

"Leave," I say.

My voice shakes.

I am not a man of violence. I am not a man of notable intelligence, either, yet I have always been able to speak to people. I cannot speak to him. This boy scares me like no one has before. There is no one around to help. My only job is to protect Michael. From this monster, I am sure I cannot.

But I try.

I fire three shots.

At such a short distance, even guided by a shaking hand and unstable body, the bullets find home, rip into the man in the doorway. No grunt of pain emits from his mouth. No cry of alarm. No blood pours onto his shirt. He stands with his arms folded. He smiles. I stare at his teeth. Then, at last, fear drives my eyes into his. I try to ask what he is.

We are in the woods.

I sit on the ground, back to a tree. My captor sits on a felled trunk. We are at the perimeter of a clearing, lit by an overlarge, silver moon. I do not know which woods. Rachael's rapist tells me his name is Thomas Q. Carlson. He flexes his muscles, sticks a thumb in a bullet hole in his shoulder.

"I think I'll leave the kid there a while," he says.

"What have you become?"

He stretches, yawns. "You meet interesting people in prison. Guys that hit cops are pretty boring. Lemme ask you something."

I do not give permission.

"You ever have a guy shove his cock in your ass?"

I am silent.

"It hurts the first time. And the next couple. Till you realize that if you just stop fighting it you might actually get to like it." He shrugs. "I never really got to liking it." He looks off into the distance. "Makes me think about what I did to people before. Thought about what makes people good, makes 'em bad. No one's much of either, really. I'm a prick, you're a prick, that girl I fucked in her apartment, she's a prick. Hell, the kid's probably already a prick. The world runs on who the biggest prick is. And in this place, right now, it's me. You catch my drift?"

"You are certainly a prick."

He lets out a booming laugh that shakes bats from their perches. He shakes his head. He says, "The mouth on you." He laughs again.

I stand, using the tree to push myself up from the ground.

He tells me to sit the fuck back down.

I begin to speak. Before I can finish a word, Thomas Q. Carlson slaps me in the face, having covered the distance between us faster than eyes could follow.

I lie face down, tasting blood. The ground is cold and hard. Blue, red, and green dots swirl on the backs of my eyelids.

"See, here, I'm the biggest prick," he says. "But I ain't the biggest prick there is."

Hardly.

"See, because there are some interesting folks in prison. A lot of darkies. Some spicks. A couple gooks that you'd be real hard pressed to cross."

All I see are the dots.

"There are a bunch of fellas like me, too. Big white guys. I tried to get in with them. Turns out they've got some rules. Like you gotta give Dodge, their leader, most of your food. I like my food. I don't wanna give Dodge any. That means I don't fit in with the fellas like me. But I ain't a darky, spick, or gook, neither. There are other ways to get in with maybe a different crew; like I said, I never much got to liking a cock in my ass. What's a guy to do, in such a situation? I'll tell you. You try to find a prick bigger than the biggest prick you can find. In prison, the only bigger pricks than the pricks inside are the pricks watching 'em."

I find the power to roll onto my side and look at Thomas Q. Carlson.

He kneels before me.

"I was a big prick on the outside. Not so much inside. They do some shit to ya in prison. For actin' up. Or just for fun. One of the things they liked to do to me for fun was this: they soak a towel in salt water, lay it from your shoulders down to your knees. Then they take this whip, a real mean fucker. It has little iron holes punched in it. Where the holes hit, ya get blisters. Then the whip pops the blisters and the salt water from the towel soaks into 'em. Hurts like a real son of a bitch. What do I do about this little situation I find myself in?"

I do not answer. He flicks me on the tip of the nose. I feel the cartilage break.

He sneers. "I asked you a question."

"I do not know."

"So I get a way to be a bigger prick. There's a night guard, well, there are a bunch of 'em, but there's one particular night guard at the pen. This fella they call Vlad. Vlad don't talk. Every now and then you hear a story about this prick, Vlad. That Vlad took someone away to confinement and no one ever saw 'em again, that sorta shit. Even with this make-believe shit, everybody knows that Vlad is the biggest prick there is outside the warden. But the warden seems to think Vlad's probably the biggest prick there is. You just know. Some guys see them together sometimes. Come back saying ol' Vlad had the warden shaking in his britches. Now I figure, okay, let me find out what makes Vlad such a prick. I know how it's done. Guys been doing it to me my whole life. Get next to the baddest wolf, make sure you don't end up a little pig." He laughs. "You know what I love about that story?"

I consider not answering. He does not strike me as patient at the moment. I ask him what.

"Pigs can't build houses. Real life, the wolf gets to waddle home with his belly full."

Blood drips from the side of my mouth. I am careful not to spit it out.

"I get a message out to this prick Vlad. Tell him I wanna chat. Vladdy comes by my cell at night. I got this cellmate, little prick, shifty guy. He's got a patch of hair missing on his forearm. Means he owns a knife. I don't like small, shifty guys. You get stabbed getting the knife from 'em and *then* you gotta kick their asses, wondering the whole time: 'How bad did he get me? Am I gonna bleed out?' So, Vladdy, Vladdy asks what in the fuck I want. I tell him he's the biggest prick around and I wanna up my status, so to say. Vladdy looks at my cellmate—guy's asleep—and stares for a while.

"Vladdy tells me he wants to taste the guy's blood. I knew Vladdy was a prick but that feels like a little much. Well, when you're the biggest prick there is, you get to make those kinds of demands. See, but I know my celly's got a shiv he made from a toothbrush hidden in his mattress. That means I risk starting shit with him at my own peril. But he's asleep, so it's pretty easy to get his blood for good ol' Vladdy. I just yank my celly up off his mattress before he knows what's what and bounce his head off the bars until there's blood everywhere.

"Vladdy reaches in with the tip of his little finger, wipes some gunk off the celly's head, and tastes it. He tells me it's the flavor he likes and that's good luck for me. Then there are all the other night guards and they're dragging me from my cell. They beat the living shit outta me. Vladdy gets me tossed in the box. I don't eat for days. I don't talk to no one. You'd be amazed how much you miss people when they're all gone. Some time goes by. Finally ol' Vladdy opens my door. I'm weak and I think I got a fever. Vladdy stands in the doorway looking down at me. He asks what I want.

"I say that he came to see me.

"He says nah, what I wanted originally.

"I tell him I'm tired of being one of the small pricks around the joint. Ask him what I gotta do to increase my size.

"He asks me what I'm willing to give up to get that. That's when I notice he's got blood dried up all around his mouth. It's a real sick look he's giving me, too. Like he's on a bender or something. He wants to know my blood type. I don't got a fucking clue what my blood type is. Vladdy walks up all casual and rips out one of my teeth. Just tears it out bare-handed. What do you think about that? You want me to start ripping your teeth out?"

I say, "No."

"No, what?"

"No, thank you?"

"Good answer."

I ask, "Is there any point to this story?"

"Oh, hell yeah. But you gotta let me get there. You gotta be *patient*. I've got all the time in the world. You should like that. See, the longer I'm talking, the longer you're living."

I swallow an entire mouthful of blood.

He looks into the distance and asks, "Where were we?"

"Vlad pulled out one of your teeth."

Thomas Q. Carlson snaps his fingers. "Right, right, right. So ol' Vladdy, he yanks out my front tooth. Holy shit, does that hurt. He puts the tooth in his mouth and rolls it around. Tells me he doesn't like A positive. Too bitter or something."

(I agree.)

"Meanwhile, I'm rolling around the floor of this cellar, holding my face, screaming bloody murder at this bastard who just ripped my tooth out.

"Vladdy tells me to shut my trap. Then he thanks me for roughing up my celly so he could sample him. Now I'm all out of my head with pain and questions, but Vladdy's just watchin'. He asks me if I want power and I tell him yeah that's the whole reason I ever even tried to get in touch with him, the prick. Well, Vladdy doesn't seem to mind the name calling, but he's annoyed anyhow. He takes me by the ankle and drags me outta the cellar. I'm screaming for help from the other guards but they're all ignoring the situation. Vladdy takes me down to the end of the hall, where there's one cell that looks a lot older than the others.

"The door's all rusted and everything and it's real dark inside. Vladdy pushes the gate open and tosses me by my ankle into the cell. Then I'm falling down some stairs and I hit my head and I've lost all my bearings. Smells awful. The floor's uneven. These rock-hard pointy pieces of something are all over the place jabbing me. Vladdy's footsteps echo down. Then I can hear him.

He lights a torch from the wall and holds it to the side of his face. I take my chance and look around.

"The jabby things are bones. There's a skull looking at me, still attached to the backbone. So I scream like a bitch. Ya know, a real high-pitched wail. Ol' Vladdy laughs this real deep laugh. He's a handsome fella—no shame in saying that. He's got bright eyes and real high cheekbones, thick head of black hair, the works. He asks me if I wanna see his face. I tell him I can see his face just fine. He laughs again and says nah, nah, nah do I wanna see his *face*.

"I'm confused as all hell, but that kind of fear makes men agree to just about anything. Suddenly ol' Vladdy ain't ol' Vladdy no more. He's this creepy fuckin' thing. The skin's all sliding and cracking off his face. The fucker even had a worm crawling through his empty eye socket. I'm really screaming now. Vladdy tells me I should be careful what I ask for, but that since I want it, he's gonna make me the biggest prick there ever was. Then he smiles and he's got fangs. I can't even hear myself screaming no more. Probably broke an ear or something. Vladdy jumps on me and bites into my neck and it's the worst pain I've ever felt in my whole life.

"Now here we are."

I ask him what he is trying to tell me.

Thomas Q. Carlson shakes his head. "Knew I shouldn't've slapped you so hard. I'm a vampire now, compadre."

A sardonic laugh bursts from my cracked lips.

"You are as stupid as I have always thought," I tell him.

He fingers the bullet hole in his shoulder. "I'm not the little prick lying there bleeding."

The rapist squats on his haunches and takes my chin in his fingers. Here's my real face, he tells me. His farm boy features vanish, replaced by decayed flesh and rheumy eyes.

"You did this to me," he says, smiling. His canines are, in fact, fangs.

I say, "You did that to you."

He stands, shrugs. "Maybe. But if I never went to prison this'd never have happened. It comes with its perks, but I ain't in love with being dead. I'm gonna tell you a little secret." He flexes dead arms in the moonlight. "Dying *hurts*. A dead body is stiff. I'd have never died if you hadn't tricked me into hitting you in front of an oinky. I never forgot that, you know."

"I didn't trick you," I say. "I warned you. What is done is done."

He answers, "And what ain't happened yet ain't happened yet."

"What is going to happen?"

"Damn. You ain't nearly as smart as you make it sound."

There is a jagged rock beside the tree. I reach for it. It is sharp enough to cut my skin. Thomas Q. Carlson pays me no mind. He stares at the moon. I know I have no hope of defeating him. I take the rock, reach it out as far as I can with both hands, and with all the strength of panic jam it back into my own Adam's apple. The flesh breaks. Air mixes with blood, rushes into my body through an unnatural hole. It hurts very, very badly, but I will not give him the satisfaction of taking my life. He will not take the power from me again.

Thomas Q. Carlson laughs a terrible laugh.

# Chapter Seven

I arrive home.

I am dirty and unshaven.

I am stiff and uncomfortable.

The porch's roof looms above me, blocking out the moonlight. But the moon's light does not harm me; it is only a reflection of the sun's past glory.

The outdoor furniture looks as though it has not been used recently. The porch has not been swept.

Rachael answers my knock upon the door. She is as beautiful as the day I met her. She throws her arms around me. She demands I get inside that instant.

"Where have you been?"

"I'm so sorry—"

"And what have you been *doing*?"

"I need to talk with you—"

"Are you okay?"

"We need to leave right—"

"Is that . . . is that blood?"

She smells like food. Her perfume is sweet. Her flesh savory.

I look away.

She takes my cheeks in her palms and makes me face her. Her eyes grow wide. "What is going on? What happened to you? Have you taken to the bottle? It's been over a month. Talk to me. Please."

"I died," I croak.

"What?"

"I died. My body is still fresh. It will not be for long."

"Oh, Lord, you're drunk. Okay. We know what to do when this happens. I'll take you to bed, come on."

I tear myself away. "I am not drunk."

Rachael stands with fists on hips. "You smell awful."

I raise my chin, revealing the gaping wound in my throat. She gasps.

"Gideon, what is that?"

I tell her I think I killed myself. I tell her I think I may have killed us both. I tell her I think I may have subjected us to the whims of one Mr. Thomas Q. Carlson for all eternity.

Whatever concern she still has for my well-being leaves her face. "Never use that name in this house."

I tell her that he is no longer in prison. I tell her that he has returned. I tell her that he is a monster.

"He's always been a monster."

I tell her that that day in the park, it was the right thing to do. I tell her I did it for her. I tell her I did my best.

She tells me that I didn't do anything for her, that what I did was for me and no one else. "You just *had* to prove you were smarter than him, didn't you? Every time someone is better than you at something you have to try to prove you're that much better than them at something else." She takes two fistfuls of her hair. "All we had to do was get up and walk away. That's it. He was out of our lives. He was gone long enough for us to almost forget him. And you brought him back."

"I was trying to get rid of him."

"But you didn't!"

She paces back and forth before the Victorian sofa. The sofa that sits directly beside the porch windows. The one that in the springtime, at 4:30 p.m., the sun shines down upon with nourishing life. A sun whose light I already know will never again touch my flesh.

These thoughts consume me.

When I come around to reality, Rachael is screaming at me. "Does he know about Michael?"

I swallow. Plasma oozes from the open wound. "Yes."

Rachael's pacing quickens. "He knows. Okay. We're leaving."

Rachael storms up the stairs shouting Michael's name.

The boy emerges from his bedroom, rubbing his eye with a knuckle.

"Mama," he says. "What's wrong?"

Rachael kneels before the boy. "We're leaving, honey. We're going. Come on."

She takes him by the hand. His pajamas are brown with blue diamonds on them. The boy does not have a strong sense of aesthetics yet.

"Papa," he asks me, "what is wrong?"

No one bothered to close the door after my return.

In the open frame stands Thomas Q. Carlson. "Howdy."

Rachael screams at him to get away. He smiles. Rachael runs to the back of the house. She drags Michael by the hand. Thomas Q. Carlson now stands in that doorframe, backlit by the moon. Rachael backs away, shielding Michael with her body. Her screams of fear turn guttural.

She shouts, "You cannot have him. You will never have him."

"Ain't ya gonna invite me in?" the rapist asks.

Rachael backs Michael into the sitting room. Thomas Q. Carlson appears in the front doorframe once more.

"It's real impolite not to invite old friends into the house."

I lurch to stand between the vampire and my family. "Go away."

He laughs. "Nah."

"I am your equal," I tell him.

"You're nothing."

I tell him again to leave.

He tells me to eat shit.

I lunge for his throat.

My movements are clumsy and imprecise. Thomas Q. Carlson is fast, having grown much more comfortable in his stiff body. He catches me by the throat. I do not feel the sting. I grab his wrist and dig my fingers into his flesh with new vampiric strength. I cannot shake him, but he cannot shake me either.

"Stay in the house," I gurgle to Rachael and our son.

They do not understand. They run.

Thomas Q. Carlson howls. He cannot go through the house. He attempts to throw me aside. The dead tendons in my flesh are just as unyielding as his. After a brief struggle, the rapist decides to bring me with him. In a moment, we are in front of Rachael and Michael. The night is bright and gleams in my family's eyes. Thomas Q. Carlson tries again to shake me. Michael whines behind his mother.

The vampire jams two fingers into my nose and rips it off. I hit him hard across the face. It breaks his grip. It breaks the hold of my other hand. I stand between him and my family. He is not breathing hard. He is not breathing at all. He laughs, then flashes behind my son and common-law wife. He takes Michael by the shoulder. The child cries out. Rachael lunges toward them.

Thomas Q. Carlson backhands her away. The trees watch but do nothing to help.

"I want my kid," the rapist says.

His words are where I find speed. I tackle him away. We grapple on the ground. Rachael takes Michael by the hand and runs further into the woods. Thomas Q. Carlson stands, hoists me by the waist, throws me sideways. I crash into a tree.

Thomas Q. Carlson walks jauntily after my family, whistling. He taunts Rachael and Michael. Rachael trips. Michaels falls with her.

"Hey," the vampire says, slowly approaching. "Your man tried to kill himself, you know. Butchered his throat with a rock. But I saved him. I'm gonna remind him of that forever. Do you know how fun breaking people is? The biggest prick makes the rules. And that's me."

Michael scoots away on his backside, trying to get behind Rachael. She shields him with outstretched arms. Thomas Q. Carlson knocks her aside and lifts Michael by his shoulders.

Thomas Q. Carlson says, "You're gonna be big someday, kid. That's all from me. You wanna live forever? I can make that happen. It'll hurt, but kids gotta feel pain sometime. Toughens 'em up. That way they don't end up like that little prick over there. I'm gonna make him suffer. Maybe forever."

*Forever*. The curse Thomas Q. Carlson places upon my head rings ominously in my ears. He sets the boy down and lays a hand atop his head. At the time, I know very little about vampires. At university, there was a class about human anatomy. There is a branch lying beside me. Thomas Q. Carlson has his back to me. He taunts Rachael. His hand is on my son's head. I take up the branch.

I run as fast as I can. I spear Thomas Q. Carlson with the momentum of death. I drive the tree branch through his back, through his heart, and out of his chest. Thomas Q. Carlson's hand is atop my son's head. Thomas Q. Carlson convulses when the branch pierces his heart. Thomas Q. Carlson's hand clamps Michael's skull.

Michael's neck snaps. Michael's head explodes from the vampire's grip. Michael dies.

Rachael screams.

Thomas Q. Carlson's fully dead body falls to the earth. My son's grey matter oozes between his fingers. Rachael hugs herself about the knees, rocking back and forth, mouth locked open in what is now a soundless scream.

✦ ✦ ✦

Margot does not react to the violence of the story. Perhaps she is so accustomed to violence that it no longer fazes her—or perhaps she has seen too much of it to want to venture anywhere near it.

She asks, "Your name is Gideon?"

"Yes."

"That's pretty weird."

"It is a Hebrew name. It means destroyer."

✦ ✦ ✦

In the coming years, Rachael retreats into herself entirely. During the night, she screams at unpredictable intervals. I do not know what she does during the day. There is only the assumption that it is the same.

She does not feed herself. She docilely accepts spoonfuls of porridge or soup. She never asks or thanks.

I decide on a change of scenery.

Rachael neither protests nor comments when I tell her we are moving.

I pack her things in the night. We take an automobile up the narrow road and around the city. There is a large Tudor house on a hill. There is no driveway leading up to the house. There are no neighbors.

I leave the automobile at the bottom of the hill and carry Rachael up the stepping-stone path to the door. I set her down on her feet. She stares into the distance. I knock. A stooped-over man with alcohol on his breath answers. I look him in the eye. His jaw goes slack. He invites us in and leads us upstairs to a small bedroom at the back of the house. Rachael, at my urging, sits on a green armchair. The room is wallpapered in roses. It has a small chest of drawers and a twin bed. There is a large closet beside the door.

My father opens a safe in the closet, removes the deed to the house, and hands it over. I ask him if the home has secrets. He shows me a trapdoor that leads to a basement beneath the basement, delving deep into the hill. I ask him if he has family. He shakes his head, mutters, "Not anymore." He follows me out back. I bite through his neck and drink the blood. I dig a hole with my bare hands. I bury the body and do not bother to mark the grave.

I check on Rachael. She is sitting in the armchair, staring into space.

I spend the nights of the next week traveling back and forth between our former home and our new one. I redecorate how I think Rachael will like it. She does not comment. I feed her when I wake, bring keepsakes and pictures to her when she does not engage in conversation.

I kill every four nights or so, when Rachael begins to look less like a companion and more like food. My meals are always large boys with broad shoulders and rough speech. I bring the Victorian sofa to the Tudor home and place it beside the window. Rachael walks down from the musty room upstairs to sit on it. I buy a coffin and put it in the subbasement. At the time, I still know very little about vampires. The coffin feels like home.

As time passes, Rachael grows emaciated. She allows me to feed her but only eats sparsely before she begins to refuse.

After two years of this routine, her eyes come into focus.

She looks at me when I bring soup and tea, mumbles things.

Each night I try to decipher the words.

One year later, I realize she is asking me to kill her.

I cannot.

Eventually, I emerge from the basement to the smell of the oven, cracked open at the top. The house is full of carbon monoxide.

✦ ✦ ✦

"She Sylvia Plathed it, huh?"

I swallow. "Yes."

"That isn't your fault, you know."

"Do you know why I never acted on her request that I kill her?"

"Dude, I'm not a mind reader."

"Because I knew I had already done so."

Margot says nothing.

She looks away. She looks back. She starts to speak.

I look her directly in the eye. Her jaw hangs.

"You will forget all of this. You will forget this room. You will forget Rachael and my son. You will be happy."

I lead her from the room. I close the door.

✦ ✦ ✦

It is Jacob.

"I threw the gun I bought in the river."

"That is excellent news."

"Why would anyone want to kill themselves?"

I'm not sure I follow.

"Life is good, man. Life is great. My boss congratulated me on an article I wrote. The client called. Said it was damn near perfect.

"Wonderful."

"Yeah. The granddaughter, by the way—"

"The smoke show?"

He laughs. "Uh huh. The smoke-show granddaughter. Super fucking into me. *She* texted *me* to hang out. Girls don't just text me to hang out usually. So she's into me. I take her to happy hour at this Mexican place. White bitches love Mexican. We drink margaritas and she says she likes sci-fi cartoons. She made a necrophilia joke, which was hilarious."

"Necrophilia is funny to you?"

"In the right context, sure. I like weird people. She's weird. She's got this tattoo of a quote on the inside of her bicep. A quote from those books where the wizard fights crime in Chicago. *The Dresden Files*. Love those books. She does too. We talked about them for a while. She says that the quote is like her credo in life or something."

"What was the quote?"

"Life would be unbearably dull if we had answers to all our questions."

"Quite."

"Yeah. So she's smart. And hot. And weird. And funny."

"You like her."

"I *really* like her."

"And she likes you."

"That's what she told me, anyway."

"You sound happy."

"I think I might be."

"I'm glad you called to tell me."

"Well, about that. That isn't really why I called. You've told me stories about two girls, right? Well, I know how you met the one, in that park with the boomerang, which, by the way, I told that story to a friend and they think you're out of your fucking mind, too. But that isn't the point. I've been working with this philosophy lately that, as social creatures, humans need to meet other humans. I know that's nothing even approaching a new idea, but it's been improving my quality of life little by little. So, I was just thinking: you never told me how you met Rachael."

"I've never told you about the best day of my entire life?"

"No."

"That seems odd."

✦ ✦ ✦

I am thirty-one again. It is an unseasonably vibrant weekend in January. The sun has found additional shine and the wind a file for its teeth. I am on the beach. The ocean is too cold to enter but still beautiful in its neverending struggle with the shoreline. I have come alone to disengage from the city's air and monotony. Jeanine always hated the beach.

My grandfather's tournament boomerang is in my hand.

(The fucking boomerang again?)

(Yes. The fucking boomerang again. May I please continue?)

I face the ocean, my trousers rolled to just below my knees, sleeves cuffed above the elbows. I have left my hat sitting idly in the white-gold sand.

I hold the boomerang vertically before me, bisecting my face. I take two small steps followed by one large, move my right arm in a wide arc, then hop and throw the boomerang as hard as I can at the ocean.

It topples end over end, rotating to the horizontal throughout its trajectory, before returning to the vertical and hooking back towards me.

Or it *would* have come back towards me.

If I had gotten better at throwing a boomerang.

The boomerang hammers into the sand five feet to the left of me and ten behind. With a sigh, I go and retrieve the toy to try again. I dance across the sand, hopping and throwing until my forehead is beaded with sweat and my back is dripping. In all this time the boomerang returns to my hand a total of one time. It is so exhilarating that I promise not to stop until I reach three.

My prospects of success do not look good. Still, I hop and throw. Hop and throw. I launch the boomerang as hard as I can, to the protest and small pop of my shoulder. I clasp the aching joint after a particularly vigorous throw that doubles me over. The boomerang arcs over the ocean and returns, unbothered by my feeble attempt to catch it. From a ways off I hear a startled gasp and then angry scuffling.

"Hey!"

I turn to see a striking girl with dark curly hair and glacial eyes. She storms over, brandishing my boomerang above her head. She is wearing a black-and-white-striped one-piece bathing suit. She kicks sand onto my feet when she stops.

"Hey! Watch where you throw this thing, huh? How old are you? I mean—"

Our eyes meet. Time slows. There is no reaction on her part other than continuing recrimination. I watch her mouth form elongated vowels, sharp consonants. I do not understand the words for some time. I observe how the angles of her face shift while she speaks.

The next thing of which I am conscious is her snapping her fingers in my face.

"Is there something wrong with you?"

I force myself to attention with a physical jerk of my body. I wince and grab my shoulder.

She asks, "Are you okay?"

I clear my throat. "Yes, yes, I am quite all right, thank you. I am very sorry about the boomerang, Miss . . . ?"

"Cross."

"Miss Cross."

"Well, all right then. Here."

She thrusts the boomerang back at me. I accept it with a smile that I hope is both endearing and innocently apologetic. She returns to her towel and dumps herself gracelessly onto it, battering the sand.

She is alone. She rolls onto her stomach, hands folded beneath her chin.

I roll my shoulder. It hurts. I decide that Miss Cross is more interesting than catching a toy. I walk over and sit in the sand next to her.

She opens one eye. "Yes?"

"Hello."

She sighs. "Hello. I would greet you properly, but you did not see fit to introduce yourself upon requesting my name."

I clear my throat uncomfortably. "Yes, of course."

I tell her my name. She awards me a surface smile with no teeth.

"So, uh, do you come here . . . a lot?" I ask.

She raises a dark eyebrow. "To the beach?"

"Well, I guess, more—" I clear my throat "—this particular beach."

She puts her head back down.

"Yes. I come here when I can. Do you need something?"

"No. No, I don't need anything. I seem to have tweaked my shoulder, however. It would be a shame to waste such a beautiful day, would it not?"

"Yes. I like to spend these types of days relaxing." She gives me a pointed look.

I say, "A relaxing day it is."

"You are simply not getting it, are you?"

I excuse myself. I begin to stammer and apologize. At first she continues to look irritated. When I get up and start to brush the sand from my trousers, however, I slip and fall back, landing hard on my rear end. Miss Cross giggles. I feel the heat rise in my face and wish the wind had just a bit more bite.

I tell her how very sorry I am, and that I will be on my way.

She says, still giggling, to call her Rachael.

She says she's sorry for being cross (a phrase that will become one of the most endearing in the world to me), but she came here to escape the city and her boyfriend for a day. She simply wishes to be alone.

I ask if she is busy next Wednesday.

She says that she is not.

✦ ✦ ✦

Jacob asks if the boomerang is like a symbol or something.

It is just a boomerang.

He asks, "And you just looked at her once and knew you loved her?"

"Loved? No. However, there are people you meet in this world that you immediately know are important. She was important. Everything that happened to us, everything we went through, for both good and ill, was important. Life is shaped by joys and pains alike. Pain is the most gorgeous thing in the world from the right angle."

Jacob laughs. "Like that song from Rob Base and DJ E-Z Rock."

It is an amazing moment of connection in my life. I love that song.

I say, "I love that song!"

With equal excitement, Jacob cries, "Me too!"

"Joy and pain," I sing.

"Sunshine and rain," he rejoins.

The two of us laugh over the phone.

He says, "It's a neat idea. My life is pretty beautiful, then."

"Jacob, a word of advice."

"Uh-huh."

"Do not let the floor fall out. You are having a good day, a good night. Focus on this. Do not begin dwelling on your pains and failures. Think instead of your joys and triumphs. The text messages you received today to make you smile. Things are looking up."

"Uh, yeah man, sure. Ya sap."

"Do you need homework?"

"Nah, I've got it under control. Peace, brutha."

Margot descends the ladder, yawning. She returns to the Victorian sofa with a copy of Dostoyevsky's *Notes from Underground*. I stare at the battered copy. Margot notices me noticing.

She affects her imitation of me. "Given our current setting," she says, "I believe this to be at least a mildly appropriate read."

In return I speak in a high falsetto. "Yeah, and like being underground is super dreary or whatever, so this old fucking fart probably has some, like, super dreary view of the world. I love dark stuff. I'm dark. I'm Margot."

She raises an eyebrow. "Margie."

"Apologies. I'm *Margie*."

"Better. Ya dick."

Two more calls follow. One is a nineteen-year-old whose parents are going through a vicious divorce. He talks for a long time about his childish ideas of true love and how he just assumed that married people had to be in love. He also notes that true love probably doesn't involve fucking your wife's sister. At least his dad kept it in the family, he tells me, laughing with fury. The other caller is a girl who was fired today. She assures me her college degree has no actual value. She isn't pretty enough to just fall into a new job. She is sick of working.

The opportunity to vent removes both of them from the proverbial danger zone.

Jacob calls back.

"Twice in one night," I say. "Aren't I just the luckiest boy in school?"

"Okay, that was a weird thing to say, even for you. Moving on. So, I told you about the granddaughter earlier, right?"

"Yes.

"So the other girl, the one I've liked—"

*Loved.*

"—for a really long time. She texted me. Can I read it to you?"

"Go ahead."

"So it reads: 'Hey Jacob, I know we've had this weird tension in our relationship and I know I haven't really been too great to you and when you asked me out I just sort of panicked. The problem now is that I've been thinking about you a lot. Something's shifted over the last day or two and I don't really want to be your friend. Not that I don't want to be friends but I want to give us a shot and I think it would be a mistake to shoot wide on this kind of opportunity. If not or if you hate me I completely understand but I wouldn't be able to sleep tonight if I didn't at least say something.'"

I say, "You don't sound happy."

"Well then there's another text right under it that says: 'I'm so sorry, I don't know what I'm thinking. You don't even have to answer that. Sorry.'"

"And?"

"And I think I should answer it," he says.

"Then the problem is solved, no?"

"But—Lucy."

"The old man's granddaughter?"

"Yeah. This other girl, Charlotte, is someone I've wanted for so long, you know? And I don't know what to do now. What if I pass on Charlotte for Lucy and that doesn't work out? Or what if I pass on Lucy for Charlotte and its ruins my friendship with Charlotte and then, like, Lucy is just gone?"

"How do you feel about them?"

"I like them both. A lot." He breathes an exasperated sigh. "Talk about fucking timing, man."

"Life is full of such inconveniences."

"Yeah. What should I do?"

"May I speak candidly?"

"Yeah."

"Choose one. Do not divide your heart. Life is an unsolvable puzzle no matter what you do. There is no need to complicate it with pieces that do not fit together."

"Okay. Should I go with Charlotte or Lucy?"

"That I cannot decide for you."

"Ugh. Some fucking help you are. Okay, okay. What do I say to Charlotte for the time being?"

"How do you feel?"

"Will you stop asking me that? I clearly *don't know*. Okay, how about this: 'Hey, of course I don't hate you, don't be silly. Obviously I like you a lot. You have nothing to be sorry for, I'm glad you told me. But there's kind of a lot on my mind right now. Would you be gracious enough to give me a couple days to think?"

"That sounds good and honest."

He huffs. "*Gracious*. Should I say *gracious*? Is it too pretentious?"

"Gracious is an excellent word."

"Definitely too pretentious. I'm gonna change *gracious* to *patient*. Yeah, *patient* is good." He rereads the text message, substituting *patient*. "Yeah, that works. Ugh. No. There's nothing cute in it. It sounds like I'm writing a business letter. How can I cuten it up?"

"'Cuten' is not a word."

"Fuck, you're annoying." His fingers snap. "Got it. Same text, but at the end I'll sign it 'XOXO Gossip Girl.' Yeah. Good."

"XOXO Gossip Girl?"

"It's from this shitty TV show. It's an endearing end to the text, trust me."

"I shall."

"All right, sorry for bothering you again. I think I've got this handled."

"Do you need anything else?" I ask.

"Nah. I'll call you if I do, though. XOXO Gossip Girl."

✦ ✦ ✦

Margot looks at me closely.

"Do you get a lot of weird fucking calls all night or what?"

"What do you mean?"

"I don't know. Like fatsoes who just wanna talk to someone cause they totally fucking reek, or like nerd guys that watch girl shows."

My eyes narrow. "Some nights, yes."

She returns to *Notes from Underground.*

The phone does not ring for some time. I pick up the fourth novel in the *Harry Potter* series, which is substantially thicker than the previous three.

"How are you liking those?" Margot asks.

"They are interesting. I like this Hermione character especially. She is insightful. But I find the red-headed boy and blond bully to be rather intolerable."

"Yeah, Ron's a jealous twat and Malfoy's the *worst*. But later on, you kind of see how they grow up and why they are the way they are, and it's, like, rewarding."

I nod, reading about something called gillyweed that allows one to grow gills and breathe underwater. I wonder how, if these children can create matter from air, they are even moderately controllable. We read in silence for a time. It is later than Margot usually stays up. The phone is silent. I put the book down and look at Margot.

I ask her who Chris is.

"This boy. He was my only friend for a long time."

"Was?"

"Yeah. His dad is a big hunter. Chris got a hold of his shotgun and Cobained himself."

"That was the night you called?"

"The night after it happened."

"I'm so sorry."

"He probably is, too." She pauses, rigid. "Can I ask you something?"

"What would make you ask such a silly question? You can ask me anything, at any time."

"Do you think . . . do you think that maybe Chris could have turned things around? You know, if he sort of gave it another shot or whatever? Metaphorically speaking, obviously."

I tell her yes.

I tell her of course he could have.

I tell her it is never too late to start over.

I am glad Rich is not there.

✦ ✦ ✦

The odor of cigarette smoke hangs in my lair. Margot is not lying on the Victorian sofa beside my desk. Nor is she upstairs in the kitchen putting Cheez Whiz on chocolate cupcakes in what she refers to as "the savory-sweet experience of a lifetime." She is not sleeping in her bedroom. She is not playing "Nancy fucking Drew around the house, bro." She is not jeering at children on the hill. She is not passed out drunk or cursing or spouting her teenage philosophies.

She is nowhere to be found.

Everyone loved will someday leave.

The girl has proved no exception.

I go to sit still and silent at my desk. I place the Bluetooth headset over Gordon's baseball cap. I wait.

The night is apparently a happy one. Suicide season is tapering off. April to early September brings fewer calls.

There is one caller tonight.

It is a girl who says she is not really in any danger.

She had a disagreement with her boyfriend about how he smokes too much weed and doesn't pay her the deserved amount of attention.

She says, "I'd kill him if I had the balls. But God didn't see fit to give me a dick, so society believes even less in me than I do."

I ask if I may tell her a story.

"What? No. This isn't about you."

She hangs up.

I finish the fifth *Harry Potter* novel and start the sixth, which, though it is not as politically savvy, I find to be immensely more entertaining and poignant.

The school's headmaster is betrayed and dies in the end.

There is the subtle loss of an immortal friend, recorded forever in language.

✦ ✦ ✦

The next night is equally quiet. I walk down the hill. The children scatter from me. I stand at the bottom and look up at the once-bright home that has long been left to decay. Vines cover the walls; years of unwiped dirt tint the windows. Tracks from children's pickup trucks and secondhand sedans crisscross the grass. The flagstones are cracked.

I walk back up and go around to the backyard.

I stumble upon a couple having sex standing up, the girl's palms pressed against the dirty back wall of the house. Their pants are around their ankles. The boy's shirt is in a heap some feet away; the girl's is pulled up over a braless chest.

I clear my throat loudly. Part of my gullet is jolted into my mouth by the force. They look at me but do not stop. The boy shouts that if I need something to jerk off to, phones have cameras these days. I consider killing them both but refrain.

The girl slaps the boy on the side of his hip. "Focus up," she says. "You're going soft again."

I go back inside, not bothering to lock the door as I usually do. The subbasement is quiet. The computer and television project no images. It has been some time since I have had cause to feel loneliness.

I contemplate the life of my father, born to an affluent Polish family that was forced to leave Europe during World War I. He fought for the United States at the tail end of the war, then watched his father live out a hardworking life that ended in murder. My paternal grandfather supposedly tried to stop the robbery of a convenience store. The robber shot him, then fled without actually taking anything.

Once, in a drunken stupor, my father told me that he drank to get on with his life. Another time he told me that it was because he felt like an alien and the liquor brought him to earth. Yet another time he said that he wished I was dead and his life was different; drinking took him to another place.

No calls break in on my thoughts.

I finish the last book about the boy wizard. The boy who killed the headmaster turns out to have been the real hero. He did everything because he once loved a girl. In the author's mind, this seems to redeem the character.

I am not so sure I agree.

There was a prophecy that said the hero could not live while the villain survived, and vice versa. I wonder if, now that the villain is dead, the boy wizard will be able to die. Or if he is cursed to an eternal life in which he watches everyone he loves perish.

✦ ✦ ✦

I awake to the blare of the television. A wave of the most immense relief washes through my body. The emotion almost reminds me of what it is to be alive.

"Hey," Margot says. "What's up?"

"You are back."

"Yeah—I, like, live here now, right?"

"I assumed you had left because you were tired of my company."

"Oh my fucking god, Confessions of a Teenage Drama Queen. Get over yourself. I just needed some fresh air."

I ask why she stayed out all night.

She shrugs.

"Where were you?"

She swallows. "I, uh, sort of made a friend?"

"A friend?"

"Yeah." She traces her scarred arm with the opposite forefinger. "He's that blond kid that plays guitar outside. All the depressing Bon Iver covers and stuff."

"I see."

"So I crashed with him, just to get a change of scenery or whatever."

"It is good that you've made a . . . friend."

"Yeah," Margot says. "I thought so, too. His name is Daniel. He's super sweet. I think you'd like him."

"What makes you think that?"

She shrugs. "I don't know. Because I like him? You're both, like, intelligent, *moderately*, I guess. And nice to me. And he likes books and stuff. I just feel like you two might get along, I guess."

"I see."

She clears her throat. "Yeah. And that being the case, I was sort of wondering if, like, maybe I could have him over here sometime?"

I find my grounding again. "Yes, of course. I would love to meet your new friend. Why don't you invite him to dinner?"

Margot's strained smile fades. "Dinner? You mean, like, us? With you?"

"Yes, you two, with me. Have you not just told me how much I would like this young man?"

"No way. He's going to think I want to be super fucking serious all of a sudden. We practically just met."

"Nonsense. Tell him it is my idea. Tell him that your guardian will make it difficult for you to see him in the future if he declines dinner."

She scowls. "And will you?"

I make my best horror-movie face.

"Ugh," she says. "Fine."

I cannot tell if her cynical expression conceals a hint of pleasure.

# Chapter Eight

I come upstairs the evening of Daniel's planned visit. The state of the house is not what I am used to.

Margot is in the kitchen with a bottle of spray cleaner and a roll of paper towels.

"Are you cleaning?" I ask.

She looks at me from the side of her eye. "No. I'm dirtying. What does it look like?"

"It looks nice."

She beams. "I know, right? Except for the doorframes you destroyed, it looks like someone actually lives here."

"Quite."

The kitchen's granite sparkles. The floors are absent of dust and litter. I walk into the dining room. The table is set with two tall candles burning. The sitting room across from it is in a similarly immaculate state. There is a ladder leaning against the front wall of the foyer. The French windows have been cleared and shined. All the carpets look vacuumed.

I walk back to Margot in the kitchen. "You did all this?"

"Yeah," she says. "Took all day. What do you think?"

"Everything looks excellent. You did not have to do this."

"Are you forgetting we have a guest tonight?"

"I am not, no."

She checks the counter by tilting her head to change the lighting. She sees a smudge and wipes it clean.

She asks me what I plan to cook for the evening.

"I am cooking?"

"Well, yeah, obviously."

"You do not believe you have learned enough to prepare dinner?"

She scratches her neck. "Um, not for this. I want things to be, like, good."

"All right. Fine. What would you have me prepare?"

She wipes down the refrigerator door, then opens it. "There's chicken in here. And I know we have some potatoes. OJ, purple stuff, soda." She sighs. "Can you make some, like, comfort food? I want it to feel sort of homey or whatever."

I think. "Yes."

"Cool. I need to go shower, I'm gross. Daniel's coming over in an hour or so."

I nod. Her feet pound up the steps. Her bedroom door slams shut. I sigh to myself, remove the chicken from the fridge, get the potatoes from the cabinet. I am unfocused but wish to be at my best for Margot's coming guest. I simmer blood and sip. It replenishes me some. Something else is missing this night, something deep in my dead guts. But it is time to cook. Introspection can wait.

I season, butterfly, and fry the chicken; I mash the potatoes with liberal heaps of butter, milk, and sour cream, adding dill for garnish. There is nothing here with real nutritional content. I look in the bottom drawers of the fridge and find raw bell peppers and baby carrots. I procured neither of these things—

maybe Margot is changing more than she lets on. I julienne the peppers, one red, one green, and one yellow, and arrange them on a serving dish with the carrots.

I can almost hear Margot saying, "Veggies without dip? What are you, some kind of fucking psycho?"

I place a small bowl of ranch dressing in the center of the dish.

The chicken finishes frying and I set it on a paper towel to catch the excess oil. The potatoes go in a large bowl. I may have made too much of everything; such is hosting. I prepare an apple crisp to put in the oven when dinner is complete.

Margot comes downstairs, perfumed, her hair straightened. She wears a loose red blouse that leaves her shoulders bare and undamaged jeans. She looks clean and well put together.

I arch an eyebrow. "You look nice."

She blushes, smooths the front of her blouse. "You think so?"

I tell her yes. Then I turn away to make sure the apple crisp's topping is properly applied.

Margot clears her throat. When I look up her left hand is on her hip. The right, palm up, makes a circular motion towards me.

"Can you do something about all that?" she asks.

"All what? Dinner is ready for whenever your guest arrives."

"I meant you."

"What about me?"

Margot groans and rolls her eyes. "Can you, like, make yourself presentable or something? Shit."

I look down. I am in a tattered dress shirt and trousers. The ensemble is faded and scarred with age.

"Yes. I see what you mean."

I proceed towards the steps.

"Put on something kind of nice!" she calls to my back.

✦ ✦ ✦

Daniel wears boat shoes to dinner. A blazer and well-worn jeans. The T-shirt beneath his coat bears the logo of some indie band, Margot informs me. Daniel shakes my hand. His grip is firm and self-assured. His hair is windswept, his features sharp and symmetrical.

I think about the type of man of whom Jeanine's parents would approve.

He presents me with a bottle of wine at the front door. It is in a brown bag. I look inside and raise my eyebrows.

"You brought wine," I say.

He looks everywhere but at my face. "Yeah," he says. "It's my favorite, I think. I haven't had too many kinds of wine, though, so who knows if it's any good."

He laughs uncomfortably, says the house smells great.

I invite him in, ask how he is doing.

"Good," he says.

He does not ask how I am in return.

I offer him a seat in the sitting room. He chooses a winged armchair. It is my favorite chair.

I say nothing but sit to his left. There are candles burning; the scents blend nicely and give the house a homey air. Daniel makes several motions that indicate he is ready to speak, then second-guesses himself. The two of us sit in an uncomfortable silence.

Margot comes down the steps, having changed her clothes again. She is now wearing the dress with the tropical print. Her makeup is different, too. There is more of it. She has done some mysterious thing to contour her cheeks.

Daniel says, "Wow. You look great."

She smiles, tries to hide it, smiles wider. Daniel's expression is one of bewilderment and admiration. He and I stand at the same time. Daniel walks up to Margot. She stands on tiptoe and kisses his cheek. He turns bright red.

I button my jacket and wait.

Margot takes one look at me and bursts out laughing.

"The tuxedo?" she says. "Seriously?"

My face twists into a scowl. "You said to wear something nice, did you not?"

She laughs and covers her mouth, nods. "I guess I did." She looks at Daniel. "My parents died and left me to the butler," she says. "What can you do?"

He seems unsure whether it is safe to laugh at this.

I clear my throat. "Shall we eat?"

The two of them follow me to the dining room, walking shoulder to shoulder. I hold out Margot's seat for her. The dining room table is meant to seat six, two on each side and one person at each end. Daniel seats himself next to her.

I tell them I will be back in a moment. I gather dinner on my arms and return to the table. Daniel and Margot are leaning close to one another, speaking softly and smiling. I set down the serving dishes.

Daniel eyes the food, coughs.

I ask him if something is the matter.

He coughs again. "Oh, it's nothing."

"What is it?" Margot asks.

Voice soft, Daniel says, "It's no big deal. I'm vegan, though, remember?"

I wonder if this means his blood would taste cleaner. Or if it would have the fart smell of cooked broccoli. Or if I would care.

I look at Margot. Her eyes go wide.

"Shit," she says. "Fuck." Her eyes start to water. "I totally forgot. I just got so wrapped up in—I mean, I meant to say something earlier, but I wanted everything to look nice, and . . . oh, god, I'm so sorry."

Daniel holds his hands up to placate her. "No, no! Seriously. Don't worry. There are veggies here. I can eat those. And I think I have a Simply Protein bar in my car or something if it's not enough." He places a hand on her shoulder. "This is perfect, really. Plus there are potatoes."

"Potatoes full of butter," she whispers.

"Right," he says. "But who cares? No harm, no foul." He turns his gaze to me. "Right?"

"Right," I say through clenched jaw. I do not like seeing Margot cry.

"Here, look." He spoons a large pile of potatoes onto his plate. He takes a bite, speaks with his mouth full. "See? It's great. This is great. I'm not, like, as strict with the milk thing."

Margot asks, "Really?"

He nods and smiles. There are mashed potatoes between his teeth. This soothes Margot.

She tells me everything is okay. She apologizes for almost making a scene. She takes one piece of chicken and one scoop of potatoes.

I ask her if that is really enough food for her "blessed metabolism" and force a smile. She gives me a pointed look.

I sigh. "You know, Daniel, I was going to prepare an apple crisp for dessert. I make it without dairy. I know it is not quite proper, but would that suit you for dinner?"

He grins. "Oh, totally. I ate gummy bears for dinner last night."

Margot smirks and giggles uncharacteristically.

I say, "Very well," and head back to the kitchen. The oven is already heated and I place the dessert within it. I return to the table. Daniel and Margot are gazing into one another's eyes. I feel like a stranger in my own home. It is not a feeling to which I am accustomed or of which I am fond.

"If you two are quite done canoodling," I say.

Daniel straightens in his chair and clears his throat. He says, "My bad."

I tell him it is fine. Margot stares bullets at my forehead. I ignore her.

"So," I say. "Daniel, tell me a bit about yourself. You've brought wine, so I assume you are a bit older than my young charge?"

He tilts his head questioningly and looks at Margot. She nods.

"Uh, yeah," he says. "I'm twenty-two. I go to the community college down the road. Tend bar at night. Just trying to figure my shit—uh—crap out, so to speak."

"Yes. I can see that."

Margot says, "Hey—"

Daniel places a hand on her shoulder. "It's fine," he says. "Really. Yeah, I mean, I'm not completely sure what to do with my life. So what? My plan is to get my associate's degree and then transfer to a four-year university."

"And what do you intend to study?" I ask.

He tells me he's thinking about hospitality management.

Margot mutters that I could maybe take a couple classes with Daniel. Daniel smirks. I take a deep, unnecessary breath.

"You are aware," I say, "that Margot is only sixteen, yes?"

All the blood rushes to Daniel's face. I have finally scored a touch. He looks over at her, his eyebrows almost touching his hairline. She stares at the table's surface, equally red. Daniel clears his throat. The habit is starting to agitate me.

Something like renewed confidence enters his demeanor. He says, "Full disclosure, I didn't know that. We met at a bar, so I guess that threw me off." He takes a deep breath.

I wonder how she gained entrance to a bar but do not ask.

There are several tense moments. Margot opens her mouth to speak a few times but says nothing.

Finally Daniel says, "It's okay. I don't mind." He takes her hand. "She's very mature for her age."

He makes defiant eye contact with me. His jaw goes slack. Before I realize it is happening, I am standing, palms flat on the table, fangs bared. Margot's chair topples backwards as she also stands.

"Are you fucking kidding me right now?" she screams.

The kitchen timer rings. The apple crisp is done baking. I come back to myself. Margot has positioned herself in front of Daniel. There is a serrated knife in her hand. I blink until I feel my dead heart, heavy and unmoving in my chest. It makes me very, very hungry. Daniel lifts his hands and rubs his eyes. Margot slams down her knife.

She hisses, "We will talk about this later."

Daniel clears his throat. "Woah," he says. "I just got super lightheaded."

"Apple crisp?" I ask, tone polite.

Daniel rubs his temples with both hands. "Actually, no, sorry. I don't wanna be rude, but I feel awful all of a sudden. Would you mind if I went to lie down for a minute?"

I tell him there are plenty of places to rest in the house if he needs to close his eyes.

Margot intervenes. She says, "It would probably be safer for Daniel to lie down at home. Don't you think?"

"Maybe that's better," Daniel says. "I'd just be more comfortable is all. I hate to leave so soon, I just feel—" He shakes his head. "Yeah. I should get going."

Margot says, "I'll walk you out."

She helps Daniel stand and escorts him to the front door.

She turns back to me as they exit, eyes alight with passion, and mouths, "Don't fucking move."

I sit, dejected, and wait.

I count the seconds that pass. Exactly ten minutes later, Margot slams the door open. She is holding her shoes. Her hair is wild, her breath short. It appears she has run back up the hill. She marches over and slams her shoes down in the center of the table, which sends the chicken flying.

"Just what in the fuck was all that?"

I say nothing.

"Oh, fuck that. You are *not* getting out of this with one of your quiet moments."

My face is wet. I did not know I could still cry.

Margot growls. "You're such a fucking pussy."

I take a deep breath, straighten my back. "He is too old for you."

Her laugh is bitter. "Coming from you? That's . . . no. You know what, fuck this. I'll be in my room, you pretentious hypocrite."

"He is a pedophile," I snap.

Margot stomps up the stairs barefoot and slams her door.

✦ ✦ ✦

Rich's new residence is not nearly as nice as the prior one. It is dirty and unkempt. The floor tiles are cracked and yellowing and the communal bathroom is covered in fecal matter. A man in a hazmat suit, hosing the bathroom down, does not notice my passage.

I find Rich in a room with an intercom outside. He is tied to what looks like a dental chair in front of a large observation window. There are sensors attached to his bare chest and temples with lines that run to beeping monitors. A security guard sleeps in a folding chair next to the door.

I walk in. The security guard does not stir. I tap him on the shoulder. He comes to and rubs his eyes. He is unconscious on the floor a moment later.

"Didn't have to hit him that hard," Rich mutters.

"This situation displeases me."

"There's a club for that."

I take the guard's chair and position it next to Rich's.

He tells me this setup is surprisingly comfortable.

I ask if he wants to be unstrapped.

He says the confinement is safer.

I ask, "Do you need anything?"

"No. You look tired."

"I do not get tired."

He looks me in the eye. His jaw is stiff. "Don't lie to me. Not tonight."

"I will do my best."

"Can't even tell the difference anymore, can you?"

"No."

He breathes deeply. "You smell like chicken."

Which makes sense.

"Blood?"

"None," I say.

"But you wanted some."

"Yes."

"You needed to feed."

"Yes."

"Lie."

"It is complicated."

"*Lie.*"

"He is taking something very precious to me."

"He hurt her?"

"He will."

Rich asks if I can keep this up forever.

"Just as long as she needs me."

He tells me it's more about me needing her.

I sigh. "It is a symbiotic relationship."

Lie.

"What do they do to you here?" I ask him.

"Experiments."

"Painful?"

"Some. Most not. Light impulses. Injections. There are worse things. Get to use the phone soon."

"Are you—" It seems like an absurd question, but I feel obliged to ask. "Are you happy?"

"I miss talking. Miss this."

"What have the doctors said?"

"They tell the truth. They say I'm helpful. Not mean. Except one. Calls me retarded, not in a medical way. He's mean. Not very professional. Could be worse."

I ask, "Then you want to stay?"

"Cameras in here."

"I will not appear on them."

"Good. What about him?" He motions to the guard with his chin.

"I assume it will appear that he fainted in his chair."

"They'll hit me."

"You would hit yourself."

He smiles. "Yeah."

"Please come home with me."

He shakes his head. "Safe here."

"Is this any sort of life for you?"

He tells me it's the only life he has. That he might as well live it while he can.

✦ ✦ ✦

Margot couldn't stand the sight of the house today, so she went back to school.

She had skipped several days, but few people notice anymore when she doesn't show up. Mrs. Deangelo wanted to know if the handsome man Margot is staying with molests her. Margot laughed in her face, asked if she could go to math class.

"And then Deangelo, the nerve of this bitch, tells me I can come live with *her* if I need to. That for some reason she feels like it's her job to keep me safe. Gives me her phone number or whatever. Says to call her if I need anything. I wish they'd just get out of my face and let me try to learn something."

John dropped Margot off here about an hour ago. She is already halfway through a large New York strip steak, a pile of heavily buttered mashed potatoes left over from the night before, and some steamed broccoli smothered in ranch dressing to make it "edible."

She avoids the topic of our disastrous evening, interrogates me about the *Harry Potter* novels. She equates herself to Harry. She once lived a desolate, abused life. Then she was taken by a benevolent person to a house full of magic.

"I guess *Beauty and the Beast* would probably be more accurate, but fuck Disney. Racist-ass, anti-Semitic fuck, that guy." She clears her throat as she gets up to leave the table. "Sorry about blowing up at you last night, by the way. I know you were just looking out for me, in your own fucked-up way."

I tell her the books were a pleasant surprise.

I tell her she could learn something from Harry.

I tell her that she, Margot, is like a bitter, vulgar Hermione.

Her eyes well up. "That is the single nicest thing anyone has ever said to me."

She wraps my shoulders in a hug. I do not know how to react. I pat her on the back.

"Okay. Ew. Um, I'm gonna go shower this moment off because now I feel totally disgusting."

She vanishes up the stairs.

I proceed to the basement, notice how nice the row of *Harry Potter* books looks on the shelf, realize Margot was right about getting the hardback editions.

✦ ✦ ✦

Vanessa is the first caller tonight.

"Hello, suicide hotline. If this is an emergency, please hang up and call 9-1-1 or go to your nearest emergency room."

She does not sound well.

"I think I did a bad thing," she says.

I ask her if she needs to talk about it.

"Yeah. That's why I'm calling. Because fuck you. I took your advice. Called 9-1-1. They took me to the hospital. They admitted me. My deadbeat ex-husband has full custody of our kids now. I panicked when I got admitted. Signed a seventy-two-hour waiver. Turns out, when you do that, they put you under psychiatric review. They fucking three-oh-twoed me. That goes on your record. Tom used it to get the kids. I guess that's better. I can't kill them now. But I miss my babies. Any mother would. My social worker says I can't see them for a while."

A gurgling choke comes through the headset.

"Vanessa," I say. "What have you done?"

"They told me I have to do an IOP. That's intensive outpatient. But they put you under psychiatric review every day. *Every* day.

They can admit me again whenever they want. That's no kind of life."

"Vanessa, I am going to connect this call to emergency services."

"Do whatever you want. The internet says I've got about three minutes left."

I conference the call. An automated message plays while I wait to be connected. Through it, I tell Vanessa that everything is going to be just fine. I tell her to please just get the treatment she needs and know there is a future. I tell her it is never too late to recover.

The 9-1-1 operator comes on the line, does his job well, demands Vanessa's address. She refuses to give it. The dispatcher tells me it will take a few minutes to find her and get a unit over. I tell him to please hurry; I will stay on the line with Vanessa. He thanks me and switches lines to take another emergency call. That is, after all, his job. Not his hobby.

Vanessa continues as if we had not been interrupted. "Tom's brother's a drug dealer. He was always in love with me. I sold him a bullshit story about my anxiety and he gave me a bunch of Xanax. I told him my back hurt. He sold me a bunch of Oxys. I bought a handle of Tito's, because you should treat yourself for your last drink."

A gurgling choke.

"Vanessa, I need you to stay with me."

"I needed to stay with my kids."

I hear the phone hit the floor.

I ask politely for Vanessa to please retrieve the phone.

I ask her to please let me know that she is okay.

✦ ✦ ✦

The police show up on my hill. The children scatter at the cruiser lights. An officer knocks on my door. Margot has been given instructions for such a situation and is lounging in my lair, no doubt biting her nails and cursing at a pirated film.

The officer asks if I can give an account of the phone call.

I invite him in.

He enters, looks around, tells me I've got a nice place. I smile with my lips, make tea. I return. The officer takes a notepad from his shirt pocket.

"Tell me what happened," he says.

"She bought prescription drugs from a dealer. She was just out of the hospital for suicidal ideation and depression and had lost custody of her children. She washed the pills down with vodka."

He nods. "Yeah, she did." He waves away tea. "Any idea why you might have been the one she called? You guys friends?"

"Yes. For quite some time."

"How'd you know her?"

The officer looks into my eyes.

"Vanessa is my niece. Not legally, I suppose. Her father and I are like brothers—or rather, we were. He passed away just recently. It has been hard on us. I suppose that, without him, I am the closest thing she has to a father."

The officer nods, scribbling notes in his tiny notepad. When he is finished, he tears the page out and eats it.

I ask if Vanessa made it.

He answers me. He leaves.

✦ ✦ ✦

Margot lounges on the Victorian sofa, doing exactly what I thought. I pluck the cigarette from her fingers.

"You're annoying."

"Pot, kettle."

"Shut up."

We sit in silence. I wait by the phone. Margot falls asleep with the television's volume up loud and several thick blankets draped over her. It is the weekend; she does not have school tomorrow. The next night, she is wearing the same clothes as before and tells me she has planned a movie marathon for the evening. She digs in her ear with her little finger.

I ask her if she feels like taking a shower and cleaning her ears properly. She ignores the advice.

She tells me, "Okay, so we've got the latest *Mad Max*—that shit is supposed to be fucking incredible. Then there's this movie with Ryan Gosling and Kurt Russell that's a couple years old but I've been meaning to watch it. Oh, and a Coen Brothers movie you should really see, because honestly, Donnie, you're out of your fucking element. Then a great one to end the night on. Have you seen *Taken*?"

She knows I have not.

"Kind of appropriate for our situation but not really. Whatever. Liam Neeson is killer with the throat chop. You'll love it. Or hate it, I don't really care. *I* love it."

She sniffs her armpit and goes to shower after all.

I am glad she is gone when Jacob calls.

"Hello, suicide hotline. If this is an emergency, please hang up and call 9-1-1 or go to your nearest emergency room."

"Well, I fucked it all up," he yells into the phone.

"Do tell."

"I didn't choose. I couldn't. I tried to have that box and eat it too. And now I'm fucked. And not in the way I like to be." He is shouting through tears. "Lucy and Charlotte found out about each other."

"You did not tell them?"

He catches his breath. "So I'm out with Lucy. She's looking fine as shit. And that day. Earlier that very day, I texted Charlotte saying we should take that shot after all. I did it all cute and everything, with an inside joke calling her Web because she loves *Charlotte's Web*. She was into it, but said she was already in for the night. I had plans with Lucy, so I lied and said I had to go out for a friend's birthday. But Charlotte had lied, too, because she was going out.

"She comes into the bar while Lucy's in the bathroom and walks up to me. It's this bar that I know Charlotte likes but I figure it's safe because she's in for the night. It turns out she got bored at home but still wanted to keep it low-key with a quiet drink. She sits next to me and I'm going into full panic mode. Lucy comes back looking hella good in these high-waisted jeans and this kind of sheer, flowy tank top. And now Charlotte eyes her up."

Margot returns to the subbasement, wearing a sweatshirt, denim shorts, and knee socks. She positions herself beneath blankets, digs at her ear.

"Lucy eyes Charlotte up. And you can just tell they both know what's going on. I'm literally sitting between them. Lucy introduces herself in that sort of bitchy territorial way that girls do when they don't know each other. And Charlotte gives it right back. Then they're staring holes in the side of *my* head, urging me to say anything at all. But I can't. Charlotte storms out, sends me a nasty text. Lucy asks who that was.

"And this is when I choose to be honest. I tell her that's the girl I'm in love with. Lucy tells me good luck with that shit and leaves. I lost two perfect women in the same night. Because I'm a fucking loser."

I tell him he is not a loser.

I say it was one night.

I ask him why he cannot simply apologize.

He says, "I've been having this fantasy all night. Praying. I know there's no God, there's just something comfortable in begging. You ever seen *About Time*?"

I tell him I have not.

"It's probably my favorite movie. This guy can travel back through the timeline of his own life, taking all his consciousness and experiences with him. He uses that power to get Rachel McAdams to fall in love with him, because not only is she the most adorable person on earth, she's totally his soulmate in this movie, like for real.

"So that's the fantasy. I've been praying for that power all night. I'd start everything over. I'd Rod Stewart my life. I'd go back to first grade. Be the smartest kid in class. Be special. Take all that time you waste as a kid and make it work for me. Develop some skills. That way I wouldn't be so fucking feckless.

"You know what? There really is no God. Equal odds for an alien-overlord science experiment put on by fourth-dimensional beings. I'm one of those people who believes there are infinite timelines. These fourth-dimensional life forms, though, they'd be what we consider omniscient and immortal. So they can see *every* timeline. The Jacob with the movie power exists, but the fourth-dimensional overlords don't have to grant me that power. Because they know what that specific Jacob, and every variation of him, is up to. They know exactly what did, is, will, would, and could happen to him at all times.

"Hell, there's a Jacob who's balls deep in Meghan Markle right now. There's a Jacob that is just Prince Harry and still balls deep in Meghan Markle right now. There's a Jacob that's getting a dual BJ from Anne Hathaway and Olivia Wilde. I'm none of them. I'm none of the good Jacobs. There's a Jacob that's in a polygamous, highly fulfilling marriage with Charlotte and Lucy. They're best-friend sister-wives. We live on a farm and talk all night and are happy all the time.

"I'm not that Jacob. I'm the Jacob who's addicted to his own sadness. Do you know what overdosing on sadness looks like?"

I do.

"You know how I threw that gun in the river? Well, I still need belts to hold my pants up."

That seems like it is probably true.

"I didn't throw those in the river."

Because his pants would fall down if he did.

"And making a noose out of them is sort of tricky but not really."

It is probably how MacGyver would choose to commit suicide. But with a rubber band and four toenails, somehow.

✦ ✦ ✦

Margot watches me curiously from the sofa, asks if I'll leave my desk to come sit with her.

I do.

"You do your best, don't you?"

"That is all anyone can do."

She leans her head on my shoulder.

*Mad Max* is high-octane nonsense. However, I admit that it is exhilarating. Oh, fuck it, it is incredible. The Ryan Gosling/Kurt Russell film is violent, but comic in the ways the characters bumble through things. By this time Margot is fast asleep.

The second film ends. Margot stirs when the final credits run. She rubs her eye, wipes her drool from my shoulder. She looks up at me and asks if a lot of people kill themselves while on the line with me.

"More than I would like."

"Why do you spend so much time talking to people like that?"

"Why do you ask?"

"I don't know, I guess. I just think that people's, like, motivations for things are interesting, you know? Like, why on earth would you wanna die with someone listening?"

I can feel her gaze on the side of my face. "Maybe it is holding onto hope until the last second. Maybe it is wanting a witness." I shrug. "All I know is that I do not like it."

She says, "Look at me."

I turn.

She stares at me with her blue, blue eyes. She removes her sweatshirt. Beneath it she wears a tight undershirt. She touches the side of my face. She leans up to kiss me.

I recoil, stand and back away.

"What?" she asks.

"Young lady. I do not understand."

She bolts up from the sofa, shivers in the cold.

"What's so hard to understand?" Her eyes fill with tears. "I'm in love with you, you stupid fuck."

Words do not form in my decrepit throat.

"Do you really not know? Do you get women *at all*? You—you're so nice to me. You cook me dinner. You listen when I talk. Look how fucking jealous you got the other night. That came from somewhere, you know. I know you say you don't like sex or whatever, but—" she motions down her body with the backs of her hands "—I'm totally fucking hot, man. Like real, honest-to-God jailbait. Some of the dudes at school go into, like, hormonal rage when they see me. Why wouldn't you want me?"

My throat flaps in a way that is almost swallowing. "For a start,

I am a century older than you."

"Age is just a number."

"But a rather important one, I have found."

"Those people. They killed themselves. And you listened. All your age and experience. You didn't save them or anything. You didn't even really try."

"How do you know that?"

She takes a small circle from within her ear. "This is Bluetooth. I've been listening to your calls."

"That is a great intrusion into the lives of others."

"Well what about you, huh? What the fuck about you? Sitting there all night listening to other people's pain. It gets you off, doesn't it? That's why you don't need sex. Listening to all those sob stories probably gets you to nut in your pants. And then you just make the calls all about you. 'May I tell you a story?' Fuck you, man. Why'd you take me from that apartment if you don't wanna fuck me? Why are you taking *care* of me?" Her tears flow freely. "What's in this for you?"

"You were in need."

"You didn't go to help those other people. The woman with the kids. That fucking nerd with the girl problems. You didn't run to save them."

Words fail me again.

"You know what? You're selfish. You ruined your own fucking life, so you have to watch while other people ruin theirs. That's it. That's it, isn't it? Just admit it."

She says my hypnotism bullshit doesn't last forever.

She says she remembers that I took her because she's the spitting image of that lady in the old photos.

She says she loves me anyway.

"The sun will be up soon," I respond. "May we please continue this conversation tomorrow night?"

She stares at me. Her cheeks are wet. She looks me in the eye. There is no sign of fear.

She storms out of the subbasement and up through the house. I listen until I hear her door slam. Then I retreat into my room, reach beneath the bed, and drag out a coffin. Something that has been dormant in me longs to see it again. I do not open it.

✦ ✦ ✦

The next night, the house is silent. Margot is nowhere to be found. Written in lipstick on her bathroom mirror are the words *Go fuck yourself.*

I go downstairs to my bedroom.

I open the coffin for the first time in over a decade.

The skeleton of the woman I love more than anything in this world or any other is inside. A woman who had eyes the blue of a glacier and a smile to melt them. A woman I would do anything to have back.

I lay down atop Rachael's bones and cry until the sun comes up.

✦ ✦ ✦

The subbasement is wrecked. The desk lies in pieces. The phone in shards. The television has a hole through the screen. The Bluetooth headset is twisted and mangled.

The Victorian sofa is unmarred. I lay on it and stare at the ceiling.

Gideon is a Hebrew name. It means destroyer.

I decide I am hungry. The next month passes in a haze of blood and shallow graves.

A drug dealer who was selling crack concealed in buffalo chicken pizzas.

A burly police officer slamming a young Black boy's head into his cruiser.

A motivational speaker spouting false promises.

The members of a neo-Nazi cell: a veritable bloodbath.

A boy who enters my home on a dare.

The perpetrators of two domestic violence incidents overheard on a stolen police scanner.

Any drunk off the street who vaguely resembles my father. One such drunk is a state judge. When I find him, he is talking to a pimp who specializes in underage boys. I take them both.

✦ ✦ ✦

Rich's asylum is truly filthy. Patients drift aimlessly in bathrobes and paper jumpsuits that zip up from the waist. Some play chess or work on jigsaw puzzles. One girl gnaws at sutured hands.

The room in which Rich was strapped is empty. I have a guard lead me to him. Rich sits pretzel-legged on his bed with a coloring book.

He smiles at me. "Hi."

I immediately begin apologizing for not being accessible to him.

Rich holds up his hand. "It's fine."

My head cocks to the side. "Yes?"

He nods. "Feel good. Have been. Experimental treatment here for severe cases. Makes my eyes hurt. But my brain feels good. Not so sad. Not so angry."

"Is that . . . is that so?"

He nods and smiles. "Nice here."

"Have you attempted to call me since last we spoke?"

"Once or twice. Figured you were busy. How are things?"

"About the same."

"Lie."

"No, it is true."

Rich's mouth turns down. "Say more."

"I don't know how."

"Lie."

I sigh. "It is the girl I adopted. She left."

"Makes you sad?"

"Very much so."

"Why'd she go?"

"Because, after all these years, I still know nothing about people."

"Not true," Rich says. "Helpful. When you need to."

I stare at the floor. "I just want to start over."

Rich touches my shoulder. I flinch. He stands up, looking much healthier than when I last saw him.

He notices me noticing, grins.

He says, "Three meals a day, plus snacks."

He tells me to stand up.

Slowly, I rise to my feet. Rich holds his arms out wide. I step towards him. He wraps me in a hug. He squeezes tight and holds me there until I lift my dead arms to return the embrace. I bury my face in his clavicle. He pats me on the back.

Very quietly, he says, "Thank you. For everything."

A nurse comes by to peek through his door. To make sure he is all right. They do this every fifteen minutes.

✦ ✦ ✦

I buy a new phone, shove the ruins of my lair into the corners. It is a landline phone with a long cord. I set it on the floor and place the new headset over my hat. I lie in wait.

A boy calls. He is standing on the ledge of a parking garage. His name is Curtis.

The drunk ones always tell you their name right away.

"I think you can totally survive a fifty-foot fall," he says. "My buddy says definitely not." He burps. "At worst I think I'll break a leg. But if I roll just right, I'll be fine."

"Curtis," I shout. "You will die."

"Nah, bro. It's chill. Life is all about jumping and falling. You just have to get back up at the end."

I sprint with all my might to the parking garage from which Gordon leapt.

I guess wrong.

I hear ambulance sirens in the distance, follow them.

Curtis lies in a pool of his own blood.

The police rope off the area. The EMTs converse quietly. I hear someone say that his blood alcohol content was probably around 0.30 percent.

People are aghast. Some cry. Others shake their heads. Lights flash atop police cruisers and ambulances.

Curtis is wearing faux-leather loafers.

His hat is soaked through with blood.

The street drinks his blood.

✦ ✦ ✦

It is a month after Curtis's wasted life. I have not left the house in that span. I decide that I need to go for a walk. Maybe I can return to the bookstore, try something more contemporary. There are fewer children on the hill. The temperate weather presents more options for activities, approved or not. The days are starting to lengthen. The nights are short. There are sports to play, long drives to be had, new adventures on which to embark. All the things I will never again have. It is about ten p.m. when I reach the hill's bottom.

Margot stands on the edge of the road.

My dead heart drops in my chest. We stare at one another's feet.

I tell her she is looking well, if a tad disheveled.

"Right back at ya."

I am at a loss for words. I am afraid.

Margot rolls her eyes. "You're so dramatic. Do you think we could go inside and, like, talk, or whatever?"

"Yes," I say in a measured tone. "Of course."

"Dope."

Margot does not walk beside me to the front door; rather, she follows in my wake. I hold the door open for her. She steps inside.

"Good to see you're keeping things clean," she drawls.

I do not wish to revisit the night Daniel came for dinner.

Margot asks, "So how are you doing these days?"

I ask if she is hungry.

"I could eat, sure."

I have kept the fresh ingredients for gnocchi gorgonzola here, replenishing the supply as needed. Just in case.

"Wow, I missed home-cooked meals. Ugh, this fucking gnocchi, man."

When she digs in, my house almost feels like home. She finishes the food in just a few minutes and belches. I conceal a smile. She rests her chin in her hands and looks up at me.

She says, "You didn't answer my question, you know."

"Which?"

"About how you're doing."

"I am fine."

She scoffs. "Good to know you haven't gotten better at lying."

"Things are the same," I tell her.

"That I can believe."

Tentative, I ask, "And you?"

Margot looks away. "Things have been better," she says. "Been worse. I don't know. Do you really wanna know?"

"Nothing would please me more."

She smiles. "Well, after you, like, rejected me or whatever—you idiot—I needed to clear my head. So I, uh, went to Daniel's."

"The pedophile?"

She rolls her eyes. "Like you don't know who I'm talking about. Well, turns out he was kind of a douche, really."

Deadpan, I repeat, "Pedophile."

"Shut up. You're so annoying. Anyway, he got drunk one night and took a swing at me."

My face tightens.

Margot tells me to chill. "He missed," she assures me. "And he keeps a baseball bat by his bed for 'home protection.' Let's just say I could have been one hell of a softball player if I applied myself."

"Atta girl."

"Yeah. Got him right in the knees. Then he just sat there crying while I collected my shit and left."

"All things considered, it is understandable he would shed tears."

She shrugs. "Whatever."

"What have you been doing since?"

She averts her gaze and clears her throat. She says nothing.

"Margie?"

"Yeah, give me, like, a fucking second to figure out what I want to tell you."

"Tell whatever you wish."

"Isn't that what I just said I'm trying to figure out?" She shakes her head. "Sorry. I didn't mean to snap." She rubs her forehead. "Things have just been weird is all."

I allow her to focus on her thoughts.

He voice becomes soft. "I've thought about coming back here a lot, you know."

"I did not."

"Yeah. So, basically, what I've been up to is homelessness, I guess. But not really? If that makes any sense."

I tell her I am sure she knows it does not.

"Fair enough. Well, I've been living sort of like those two kids in *The Hideaways*. Ever seen it?"

I furrow my brow.

"Right," she says. "Of course you haven't. It's an old movie where two kids run away and hide in a museum to live there."

"You've been living in a museum?"

"The school. It's not too tough. They don't do, like, a great job of maintenance there. It's easy to avoid the custodial staff. I stole some keys. I sleep in the nurse's office on the cots they have for when kids need to lay down with faked headaches or whatever. I wash myself in the emergency showers in the chem lab—the gym showers are nasty. I steal food from the cafeteria. Honestly, it's not the worst setup."

"It does not sound ideal."

"Did I say it's ideal?"

"You are rather grouchy today."

She rolls her eyes. "It's a day that ends in *y*, isn't it?"

I chuckle.

"There ya go," Margot says. "I kind of missed that sound."

"That is nice to hear."

She swallows. "But anyway, the school. I think they might be onto me or something. Deangelo is totally sniffing around my crotch, figuratively speaking."

"Is that so?"

She takes a deep breath. "Yeah."

"How long have you been coming to the hill?"

The shadow of a smile plays over her features. "I'm that transparent, huh?"

"It is hard to lie to the people who know you well."

The smile shows in full. "Yeah, it is. So, anyway, I was wondering if I could, like, possibly move back in?"

"I will have to check with the manager to see whether or not there is a vacancy."

"Ugh, fuck off." She jumps up from her seat. "Would it make you too uncomfortable if I gave you a hug or whatever?"

I hold my arms out. She leaps to embrace me.

"Thanks," she says.

I tell her most of her things are still upstairs.

"Cool. Do you mind if I get a long hot shower and then go to bed?"

"This is your home. You may do whatever suits you."

She runs up the steps. The bathroom door slams shut. The shower runs.

I go to my lair and shut the trapdoor behind myself. In my bedroom is an emaciated man. The judge. He is alive but in poor health. The pimp has been dead for weeks. I tell the judge he has a chance to regain his freedom. His eyes are hooded, but I can tell there is a glimmer of hope there.

I say, "But only if you cooperate with me."

"Anything," he rasps. "Anything, if you'll just please let me go."

✦ ✦ ✦

The next night I emerge from my lair. I make sure to lock the door behind me; it would not benefit Margot to discover I have backslid into old behaviors. It would be a poor example for her.

I walk into the kitchen. It smells of the oven and for a moment my mind races back to Rachael.

But Margot, very much alive and wearing oven mitts, is busy pulling a loaf pan out of the oven.

Weak with relief, I ask when she learned to cook meatloaf.

She tells me she's not a moron and knows how to Google shit. "Besides, you made this for me once, and I watched."

I remember. "But I did not teach you to make it."

"It's not exactly rocket science." She sets the meatloaf down on the stove and removes the oven mitts. A worried expression crosses her face. "You don't have any of those Tupperwares full of blood in the freezer."

"I am glad to see you cooking for yourself," I tell her.

She gives me a long, serious look. It is not a trusting look, but it becomes a forgiving one. She chooses not to ask any further questions about my diet.

"We had this nutrition unit in science class," she says. "Makes me think twice about eating—what do you call it, *garbage food*? That's hilarious, by the way."

"Why, what would you call it?" I ask.

"*Junk food*," she says. "Because that's what it's called."

We talk at length about her day and *Harry Potter*. She tells me my fan theories are old news; they've been circulating the internet forever now. I shouldn't say them to anyone who really loves the series without giving credit to the source or "they'll blow you the fuck up."

Margot yawns. It is about eleven-thirty. She says she's tired from all this paying attention. She asks if it's okay if she goes to bed, or do I want her to come hang out in my lair.

I tell her that a growing girl such as herself needs to get a good night's rest.

She goes upstairs and closes the door softly.

My first errand of the night is going to see Guy. I reject a meal from an Alzheimer's patient. I have enough problems of the brain. I accept two universal donors: bland meals, but fine. There is a vegan. I decide that I will try it, after all. I go home and place ten tubs of blood in the freezer.

I go downstairs.

The judge has been subsisting on dried cereal and jugs of water. He asks me if I'll please, for the love of God, let him go.

I tell him yes, but I need something in return.

"Please," he begs. "No more blood. I'm so tired."

"No more blood."

I unchain him and hoist him up. He drapes an arm over my shoulder.

I tell him to be quiet going upstairs, promise to end his life if he is not. He nods and I mostly carry him through and out of my home.

We need to go to his office. His keys are at home, though. I ask him for the first time if he has a family. He tells me he has two children, both daughters, and a wife. He wonders aloud about police investigations. If they've dug into his life. If they've found his secrets squirrelled away throughout the house. His child pornography and the like.

I do not care one bit.

He directs me to his home.

It is a large suburban house. The lawn is well tended, with bushes sculpted to look like animals in front. The lamp outside the door is lit. An old signal that visitors are welcome, though I believe that the original meaning has been lost. Now, lamps are lit to ward off unwelcome visitors.

I take the judge to the front door. He tries the handle. It is locked.

"Knock," I tell him.

He says he doesn't want to wake his wife or children. He is not in a good state.

I ring the doorbell until I hear footsteps from within.

A woman in a bathrobe opens the door. Her eyes are bloodshot with dark circles underneath. Her expression is harried. She looks at her husband and her eyes go wide.

"Oh, my God. Brendan? Is that you? My God! Thank you! Thank you, Lord!"

She invites us in.

I set Brendan down on their sofa. His wife makes coffee and shouts up the steps for the children to come down. Their father is home. I make up a story about finding him on the side of the road, seeing his address on his license. She says she needs to call the police and let them know her husband's been found. She shouts up the steps again. I follow her to the phone and tap her on the shoulder. She looks me in the eye. I gently replace the phone in the cradle and tell her to have a seat with her husband.

Children's feet hammer down the stairs.

"Daddy!" they cry. They jump on their father. Brendan wraps them in a weak hug. Based on their reactions, I believe Brendan's secrets are safe.

"Children," I say. They make eye contact with me. Their expressions are very innocent. I wonder how long it will be until that light leaves their eyes.

I make them repeat the story of how the judge simply returned to the front door tonight.

I make the family forget all about me.

I make Brendan get his office keys. He stumbles on the steps. His family sits on the sofa, staring into the distance. I do not tell them about Brendan's hidden life. Instead, I tell Brendan that in one year's time, he will "accidentally" send evidence of his crimes from his work email. In the meantime, he will send money to charities for children who are victims of abuse. He will harm no more children. He will live a chaste and uneventful life. After that, Margot's emancipation will be far enough in the past to garner no notice.

If he is not properly prosecuted, I will return.

I do not tell him this last fact.

Brendan directs me to the courthouse. I make the building's guard escort us to Brendan's office, tell him not to ask questions. Brendan sits behind a large, varnished desk and runs his palms over the surface.

I tell him he needs to sign paperwork for the early emancipation of a minor.

He nods but says he does not have the documents.

I tell him to write them.

He says that isn't really how it works.

I say that he needs to find a way. To perform whatever fraud he needs to within a reasonable period of time or whatever. I say that things will become very unpleasant for him if he does not. I say that the lonely room is still there.

He gulps. I tell him I will return in one week's time to collect the documents. Then I take him home to his slack-jawed family.

Margot is snoring loudly. This is good.

My phone does not ring. It has not rung for a long time. I fall asleep looking at Rachael.

✦ ✦ ✦

Margot had a good day at school. She does not have very much to tell me. I say this is a good thing. I tell her that I think, possibly, she may deserve a cell phone.

She says, "Don't fuck with me, Sean. Not you."

"My name is not Sean."

"You're so lame. It's *Good Will Hunting*."

"Oh, of course, I should have known."

"Shut up, nerd."

I tell her that was rude.

She responds that consistency is important.

We go to an electronics store together. It is next to the bookstore. There is an entire section for cellular devices. They ask about my credit rating; I look the employee in the eyes and hand him enough cash for two cell phones. He sets up prepaid service under Margot's name. I tell her I will find out how to arrange some sort of credit card so that she can pay her own bills online.

Her eyes are glued to the device the entire walk home.

She says over and over how fucking cool this is. She tells me this version of the phone just came out. She exclaims how that cunt Ashley Freemont doesn't even have one yet.

I tell her how pleased I am that she is pleased.

"Oh! Here, what's the number on your phone? We'll be each other's first contacts."

She programs my number into her phone and calls me. She creates a contact for herself on my device. She makes her name "Large Marge" and puts an emoji of a black heart and a drooling face. She accompanies me to my lair.

For the first time in a long time, the phone rings.

It is Jacob.

"You are alive?"

He says yeah, he's alive. Luckily his neck didn't break. His roommate found him before he'd finished asphyxiating. He has a wicked scar from the attempt, though.

He says, "I'm just calling to let you know everything's okay with me."

"That is the most wonderful news I have heard in quite some time."

"Thanks, man. I was in the psych ward for a while, hence you not hearing from me."

"How was that?"

"Pretty good, actually. Eye-opening, for sure. I'm seeing this psychiatrist twice a week. He's a really good guy. We've got me on a really effective drug cocktail. It's keeping me nice and level. Plus I'm doing a DBT group—that's dialectical behavioral therapy—every Wednesday night. It's a class where they teach you how to cope with the shit that gets you down for no reason. I met a girl in there. I didn't even fall in love with her the first time she said hi to me."

"Jacob, you have no idea how pleased I am to hear that."

"Thanks. That's actually not why I'm calling, though."

I ask what the purpose of the call is.

He says, "I'm calling to tell you to disconnect your phone. You aren't qualified to be doing this shit. You have no training. You're sort of, at best, an emotional crutch. Not sort of. You are. I need to stop hedging all my statements." He takes a deep breath. "If you care about the people that call you, at all, you'll stop."

I repeat that I am glad he is doing well. He hangs up. Margot does not look up from her math homework.

Jacob's words encompass my consciousness. I unplug the phone and sit in silence.

✦ ✦ ✦

The next evening, Margot informs me she is going to a new friend's house for dinner. A girl name Marianne who is also an outcast.

"We bonded over a podcast," Margot says. "It's a horror-comedy podcast. *Last Podcast on the Left*. It's so fucking funny. You should give it a listen." She stretches, checks her phone. "It's John," she says. "He's my ride. I'll be back later. Probably around ten, ten-thirty. I'd say don't wait up, but I guess you don't really have a choice, huh?"

I smile. Margot departs.

✦ ✦ ✦

Tonight is the night that begins the rest of her life. I know that. It does not make the acceptance much easier.

I go to the room that holds my antiquities and remove the new lock. The house is no longer mine. I take the deed to the house from the old, rusted safe in the closet.

I carry it downstairs. From the pocket of my trousers I take Margot's official emancipation and I place the documents together on the table. I begin to write a note about how I am only ever a phone call away.

I scratch it out, throw it away, start again.

In the new note I tell her that the house is now hers and she should keep the deed somewhere safe. I tell her that she does not need me—that she never really did. She will gain more from navigating life on her own than she ever could from listening to an emotionally unstable corpse with an unclear vision of reality.

I write that she has my phone number and that I will always answer if she calls.

I write that I will be sure to visit from time to time.

She will have to invite me in.

I sign the note with all the love my heart can still muster. I leave it with the other documents and walk down the now-deserted hill into the night.

Because it is never too late to start over.

## The Author Would Like to Thank

Christine Neulieb and Amanda Thomas, for making this book possible and ten times better than it initially was.

Stephanie Feldman, Dick Wertime, and Chip Delany for the invaluable lessons they teach.

Richard, Abbie, and Philip Katz for their unwavering (if insanely aggravating) support.

The entire Yardley Run crew for too many reasons to list.

Also, you, the reader. Thanks so much.

Photo Credit: Tina Tedesco

## About Andrew Katz

When not reading and writing fiction, Andrew enjoys puppers and doggos, black coffee, hiking, and writing bios that read like poorly made dating profiles. He is also the proud owner of several paintings that he painted himself and now hides from the world because they're bad. He lives and works in Philadelphia, PA.

CPSIA information can be obtained
at www.ICGtesting.com
Printed in the USA
LVHW011707140119
603847LV00005B/581/P

9 781941 360200